# The Deep Freeze of Bartholomew Tullock

# The Deep Freeze of Bartholomew Tullock

Alex Williams

PHILOMEL BOOKS / WALDEN MEDIA®

PHILOMEL BOOKS
A division of Penguin Young Readers Group.
Published by The Penguin Group.
Penguin Group (USA) Inc., 375 Hudson Street, New York, NY 10014, U.S.A. Penguin Group (Canada), 90 Eglinton Avenue East, Suite 700, Toronto, Ontario M4P 2Y3, Canada (a division of Pearson Penguin Canada Inc.). Penguin Books Ltd, 80 Strand, London WC2R 0RL, England. Penguin Ireland, 25 St. Stephen's Green, Dublin 2, Ireland (a division of Penguin Books Ltd). Penguin Group (Australia), 250 Camberwell Road, Camberwell, Victoria 3124, Australia (a division of Pearson Australia Group Pty Ltd). Penguin Books India Pvt Ltd, 11 Community Centre, Panchsheel Park, New Delhi—110 017, India. Penguin Group (NZ), 67 Apollo Drive, Rosedale, North Shore, 0632 New Zealand (a division of Pearson New Zealand Ltd.). Penguin Books (South Africa) (Pty) Ltd, 24 Sturdee Avenue, Rosebank, Johannesburg 2196, South Africa. Penguin Books Ltd, Registered Offices: 80 Strand, London WC2R 0RL, England.

This book is published in partnership with Walden Media, LLC. Walden Media and the Walden Media skipping stone logo are trademarks and registered trademarks of Walden Media, LLC, 294 Washington Street, Boston, MA 02108.

Published in Great Britain as *The Storm Maker* by Macmillan Publishers, Ltd.


Published simultaneously in Canada.
Printed in the United States of America.
Design by Richard Amari.
Library of Congress Cataloging-in-Publication Data
Williams, Alex, 1969–[Storm maker] The deep freeze of Bartholomew Tullock / Alex Williams. p. cm. "Published in Great Britain as: The storm maker, by Macmillan"—T.p. verso. Summary: In a land of never-ending snow, Rufus Breeze and his mother must protect the family home from being seized by tyrant Bartholomew Tullock, while sister Madeline and her father, an inventor of fans that are now useless, join forces with a ne'er-do-well adventurer and his blue-haired terrier, hoping to make some money. [1. Adventure and adventurers—Fiction. 2. Weather—Fiction. 3. Fans (Machinery)—Fiction. 4. Inventions—Fiction. 5. Dogs—Fiction.]
I. Title. PZ7.W65573De 2008 [Fic]—dc22 2008002663
ISBN 978-0-399-25185-6
1 3 5 7 9 10 8 6 4 2

# The Deep Freeze of Bartholomew Tullock

# Prologue

# 20 Years Earlier

Long ago the sun shone down on an orchard where children were painting. The apple trees swayed languidly in the heat, throwing dappled shadows across a dozen easels. Mrs. Solana, a woman with pale gray, twinkly eyes, walked from canvas to canvas, nodding with gentle approval at the crude but happy pictures of sunsets, flowers, giant butterflies. Suddenly she paused at one of the easels.

"This is interesting," she said. "Come and look at this, everyone." The children gathered around the canvas and gasped with astonishment. The picture seemed so real even though the image was alien to them—a town lying underneath a thick blanket of white.

"Philip Breeze is really using his imagination." Mrs. Solana tilted her head to one side and then the other. "Tell them what it is, Philip."

"It's snow. I read about it once," Philip replied, his gold-flecked eyes bright with interest.

"Yes—snow," Mrs. Solana repeated, as though the word held some weight and mystery she could not fathom.

"It's very, very cold apparently," Philip added.

"So I've heard." Mrs. Solana laughed. "Your father wouldn't like it much then." She was about to usher the children back to their seats when Elizabeth, a pretty girl with long red hair, stepped forward, her green eyes glowing.

"It's like something from a dream," she whispered.

Philip flushed as Elizabeth smiled at him. A sour-looking boy, Bartholomew Tullock, watched this exchange with narrowed eyes. His clothes were more formal and expensive than the other children's, and as he watched he fingered his tight, starched collar with frustration. Then, when Elizabeth's pretty freckled nose was no more than an inch from Philip's canvas, Tullock obviously could bear it no longer. He lunged forward and slammed a fist straight through the picture, then flung it to the ground, panting with rage.

Elizabeth stepped back, and the gaze she turned on Bartholomew was icy. For a moment he seemed to falter, but then his sullen glower returned.

He leaned over a stunned Philip. "I will break you, Windy. Hear me?" he sneered. "You and your family." Then he took one last look around at his classmates' aghast faces, gave a choked little laugh and ran off.

ONE

# Strange, Shining Things

Showers of golden sparks were reflected in Madeline Breeze's welding visor. Eleven years old and tomboyishly scruffy in her worn dark trousers and brother's too-big shirt, she was joyously lost in her work. Her brother, Rufus Breeze, a couple of years older and a world more tidy in his dress, stepped back from their workbench where he had been drilling holes in a piece of sheet metal and took off a pair of goggles. He straightened his carefully parted light brown hair, adjusted the sun-shaped cuff links on the sleeves of his cream shirt and tapped his sister lightly on the shoulder.

"Hey, frost-face," he said. "Hope you're not making the joints all lumpy. This thing is meant to be delicate."

Madeline flipped up her visor as she put down her blowtorch and held up the intricate metal framework she'd been working on. It was beautiful—its lines as true as arrows.

"Does this look 'lumpy' to you?" she asked, pushing

her strawberry-blonde hair away from her shiny face, leaving an oily smudge on her forehead as she did so. "But your holes are a little wonky," she teased. Rufus's face fell. "I'm joking, Rufus. Your work is always as perfect as snowflakes."

The children were working in a corner of the living room of the Breeze family house. It was a remarkable dwelling. Decorative wood-paneled walls carved with scenes of hot summer days, picnics and kites, stood in peculiar contrast to the snow falling heavily outside. The glow from the fireplace mingled with the soft light from gas lamps to illuminate curtains and rugs that although once heavy and opulent, were now threadbare and tatty.

And this room, along with all the others, was sparsely furnished—as though selling off items of furniture to raise money for food had become a regular occurrence. Worst of all, even the fire's warmth was not strong enough to banish the cold gusts of blizzard that found their way in through every crack around the windows. Rufus and Madeline could not remember a time when it had not been so. Though their parents often told them that once, as the paneled walls suggested, there had been sun in the world, sometimes Rufus and Madeline found it hard to believe. It seemed to them that it had always snowed in Pinrut.

The most remarkable thing about the Breeze household was, however, none of these details—it was the strange, shining things hiding in the shadows: piled high on shelves, crammed under the stairs and wedged into every nook and cranny. There were hundreds of them, every one different, their sharp edges and curved cogs catching the light all over the room. Even as Madeline and Rufus worked, one of them whirred out from a corner, flitting past Rufus's ear like a large silver moth with colored glass wings, wafting air in his face as it did so. But Rufus barely noticed, for at that moment his mother, Elizabeth Breeze, swished into the room. She shivered as the silvered insect flew on toward her and swatted it out of the way with a grumpy flick of her hand. Her bright green eyes took in the fevered industry of her two children, and a frown disrupted her otherwise elegant features. She gave a little heartbroken sigh.

"I thought you were going to have an evening playing like normal children. Anything but more welding and drilling."

"Father says this is what we Breezes do—what Breezes have been doing for decades," Madeline reminded her, firing up her blowtorch again. "Everything else is just frosting."

"Your father's got a lot to answer for," Elizabeth said. She glanced at the ornate grandfather clock that sat near the door. "And where is he? He's been gone for hours."

• • •

At that very moment their father, Philip Breeze, was in fact clinging to a cliff face as a raging blizzard howled around him. His face was almost blue with cold, but his hazel eyes were still warm with flecks of brilliant gold. His woolen jacket and climbing trousers whipped against his limbs as the high winds buffeted his body. Philip had been climbing for many hours now, and the cold had permeated deep into his skinny frame. But he barely felt it. He had heard about a small deposit of a rare metal in the cliffs to the southwest of Pinrut, and he was determined to find it. His wool-swathed hands reached up and grabbed the lip of a narrow rock ledge, and he heaved himself over and sat down heavily. The snowstorm was so dense he could see nothing but a churning white mass all around him, but he knew the town of Pinrut was out there, far, far below.

Philip tried to remember what it was like to enjoy the warmth of the sun, but the cold wind tore his golden memories from him, turning them blue and fragile. He shivered. And to think he had once thought snow was beautiful! Still, the sun would return soon. It had to. And he had work to do therefore. He surveyed the rock face behind him, and suddenly his heart gave a little leap. A vein of scarlet glistened in the rock above his head. True, he couldn't find his own socks in the morning—but passion and endurance had led him to his prize this time.

With a triumphant grunt, Philip pulled a pickax from his leather toolbelt and began hacking at the ore contained in the cliff.

A long, long way east from the busy Breeze family, near the settlement of Pluverton, Sebastian Silver was running for his life through a torrential downpour, with a dog clutched to his chest. From his wide-brimmed hat and butter-colored cape, to his scarlet waistcoat and breeches, he was sodden. The dog in his arms, a blue-haired terrier of much brain—and less courage—whimpered as what looked like a carving chisel hurtled past them. "I'm running as fast I can, Mesmer!" Sebastian grunted at him. He looked back over his shoulder, and his eyes widened with horror as he took in the fifty angry townsfolk gaining on them. "People are so touchy around here," he added as a large wooden mallet whistled past his ear, and he put on another burst of speed.

But eventually even Sebastian had to admit that his boots were filling with cold water and the bog beneath him was getting boggier.

"Ah, fickle fortune! I can't outrun them. I shall have to outtalk them," he muttered at last, and he turned to face the fearsome horde. The villagers' faces were flushed with anger. Sebastian hugged Mesmer closer as the rain continued to lash at them viciously. "Is that your heart beating alarmingly fast?" he hissed in the dog's ear.

Mesmer gave a low, disdainful snuffle.

"Oh, it's mine, is it? Excellent."

The crowd splashed toward them menacingly. Mesmer bared his teeth.

"Do I take it there is some dissatisfaction with the tools I sold you?" Sebastian began. "It's just that I'm not an expert, but hurling them at someone's head is probably not the best way to actually make anything."

Sebastian recognized the village leader as he waded to the fore.

"You can stop with all that highfalutin' wit and stuff," grunted Elder Sourflood, before splashing closer so that he loomed threateningly over Sebastian. He was enormous and hairy and wearing a large tin bucket on his head. Rainwater cascaded off it like a waterfall and would have fallen clear of his wet woolen clothing altogether had he not had the most gigantic barrel of a chest.

"These tools are shoddy and about as much use to us as a paper umbrella!"

Sourflood held up a handsaw even as the blade fell out of it and plopped into the water around his ankles.

"I didn't make them," Sebastian said.

"Yeah, well, you dripping well sold them to us!" exclaimed another member of the crowd, who had a clockwork device strapped to his face with an arm that flicked back and forth batting water droplets from the end of his nose. "And you knew how useless they were—no wonder we caught you trying to sneak out of town at the break of dawn . . ."

Sebastian rolled his eyes. "I suppose you want your money back."

"No, we want some good, decent tools," Elder Sourflood said. "The rains here been lashing down for the past fifteen years, and we need to keep our town up on stilts and the roofs watertight; otherwise we'll all have the rotten-foot."

"How about I go away, find some improved tools and then come back?" Sebastian offered.

"All right, go fetch us new tools, but you *better* come back," another muscle-bound crowd member agreed. His particularly bushy eyebrows appeared to have knitted together loosely to form a mesh above his eyes, keeping the water out.

"Of course I'll return. Don't you trust me?" Sebastian boomed at him indignantly.

"It's just that you better be quick about it. You're our only hope this late in the day," Sourflood said. "The heavy rains start soon and we need to get repairing. We're sunk otherwise."

Sebastian looked up at the torrential deluge of water that was falling out of the sky. *Heavy* rains, he thought to himself. What would *that* be like?

"I bid you farewell then and shall return forthwith," Sebastian said. He turned away quickly to hide his gleeful grin. Now if he could just get away quickly before they—

"Not so fast," Sourflood growled. "Do we look stupid?" Sebastian turned back. He surveyed the population of Pluverton—with their knitted eyebrows, clockwork nose-drip flickers and the buckets on their heads—and decided it was best not to answer that question.

"Give us our sodden money back." Sourflood held out a large, meaty hand. Grinding his teeth, Sebastian slapped the bag of coins into the elder's moist palm. Mesmer gave a sad whine.

"Till again we meet," Sebastian intoned over his shoulder as he walked away.

"Soon!" Sourflood boomed after him.

"Or not," Sebastian whispered to Mesmer without a backward look.

TWO

# Their Father's Obsession

Philip Breeze finally threw the front door open a few hours later and staggered into the room, grinning from ear to ear. A flurry of snow billowed in with him.

"Hey, I've got it! I've got the vendilium metal!" he cried, holding the canvas bag aloft with triumph and kicking the door shut behind him.

Madeline ran to her father and hugged him.

"You can use it to make the best one ever!" she exclaimed.

"You know, Sunshine, I think I just might," Philip said as he handed the metal deposits to an eager Rufus to examine.

"And remember, the things we make—it's not enough that they work. We must also make them special. Breathe beauty into them," their father added, removing his snow-laden coat.

"You're bleeding, Philip!" Mrs. Breeze exclaimed suddenly.

Philip looked down. His knee was wrapped in a blood-soaked piece of cloth. He looked up again sheepishly.

"I, er, tripped."

Rufus and Madeline exchanged a troubled look as their mother frog-marched their father toward a small door on the far side of the room, her long green velvet dress swishing as she went.

"When the sun arrives, we'll be rich both here"—Philip touched his temple as his wife continued to drag him across the room—"and here." He clamped his fist to his chest.

Rufus and Madeline repeated the movement—finger to temple, fist to heart—and Philip beamed at them shortly before he was whisked into a small storage room and the door slammed shut.

Strange workings, rods and springs, were embedded into the walls of the tiny room, behind the mops and buckets. Over the years before he died Rufus and Madeline's grandfather had worked hard on the Breeze home, his creative genius ensuring that it was like no other. Although he had died just before Rufus was born, his presence was still felt throughout their home with great affection.

But this evening, their father would have no time to dwell on this fact. As they pressed their ears to the wood on the other side of the door, Rufus and Madeline could hear their mother's heated tone.

"Tell me you didn't go to that cliff face again!" she was demanding in a fierce whisper.

"I don't want to lie to you, Lizzie . . . ," their father replied awkwardly. "You know, you look very pretty when you're angry. The glowing eyes, the flushed cheeks. And good job—must be terrible to be shouted at by an ugly bug every day."

Elizabeth did not laugh. Philip could be so charming and his passion and belief so lovable . . . but she had to get her point across this time.

"I suppose you cut your knee climbing down?" she went on.

"Not exactly, more *falling* down. In fact, on the bright side, this could have been a lot worse."

"Philip, this has to stop." Rufus and Madeline hated it when their parents went into the mop-and-bucket room. The voices would get louder and louder, and, left outside, Rufus and Madeline would get a sick feeling in their stomachs. They understood their mother was worried, but if only she could be proud of their father's great skill and passion, the way they were! And they understood their father's focus—almost to the point of distraction—but if only he could say the right thing, just this once . . .

"You used to admire what I created," they heard their

father say now, as though mirroring their thoughts. "You said what I did was beautiful."

"That was before . . . ," their mother replied. "Any moment we'll have that ogre Tullock banging on the door demanding payment again! And we haven't got it! Can't you see what's happening? Our family is going to be *destroyed* because of your obsession."

On the other side of the door Rufus swallowed hard, then smiled weakly in an attempt to reassure his wide-eyed sister. But he had never heard their mother sound so harsh. Things must be bad.

"That's not true! My 'obsession' is going to save us!" their father yelled back.

"Please, Philip, find another way . . . for all our sakes." Elizabeth's voice was so quiet and sad now, they could barely hear it. "We need money for food, for clothes . . ."

Philip pushed the blueprints in his head aside for a moment.

"You and the children are everything to me . . . ," he started.

Inside the tiny room, Elizabeth raised her head, her eyes brimming with tears. The corners of her mouth lifted in hope.

". . . But there is no other way," he finished. "This is what we Breezes do."

Rufus and Madeline fled to their workstations and tried to look busy as their father pushed his way back into the bare living room. Their mother stepped out behind him and watched him lift the heavy wooden door and descend into his underground workshop. As he climbed downward, she felt her heart sink too.

THREE

# A Secret under Lock and Key

Philip's underground workshop was crammed with tools. The glow from the gaslight made them glitter like jewels. He slumped down onto a wooden stool and dropped the canvas bag of vendilium metal on his workbench, the desire to create momentarily gone. When he felt this low, and it seemed to be more and more of late, he always found it motivating to let his thoughts drift back to the last time he had spoken with his father, kneeling at his bedside, more than a decade before. His father's once strong and determined face had been gaunt, his skin pale and covered with the strange snowflake-shaped bumps that indicated Pinrutian flu.

Clement had been a brilliant, energetic man, but now that life force was ebbing away. A bitter draft had seeped in around the nearby window, disturbing the candlelight and throwing sharp, twisting shadows onto the walls.

"I'm sorry, boy," Clement had whispered under his breath.

"For what, Father?" Philip said.

"When the snow came and business went bad, I . . . I was forced to borrow money from the Tullocks—just to put food on the table. Ironic, really." Clement coughed and wheezed as he fought for breath. "I thought if we just held out . . . but no—the snow keeps coming. Now we can barely make the repayments and . . . they could take our house . . ."

Philip could barely breathe. No—this was *their* house. The Breeze home. His father must be mistaken. Apparently not.

"That young Tullock, Bartholomew, he wants to destroy it. He wants to destroy Pinrut as it used to be altogether. He wants his house to tower over all, his wealth and happiness to be paramount."

Philip knew his father's words were true. Bartholomew had been a bully at school and he'd grown up to be a tyrant—made worse by the fact that since the snow began, the wealthy Tullocks' hold over poorer Pinrut had grown immeasurably. Philip hardly recognized the place and people in it anymore.

"I shouldn't have kept this from you, but you and Elizabeth have a child on the way and I didn't want to worry you . . ."

Philip struggled to make sense of what his father was saying. They were no longer safe in their own home.

"But listen, my boy," Clement continued. "The sun

*will* return soon now. It must. The Breezes will flourish in Pinrut once more. Keep on making them, Philip. Make them well. Pay off the Tullocks. Money is the only thing they understand. Buy this house back." Clement gripped at the bedsheets as a spasm of pain racked his chest.

"I will make them well, Father," Philip said even as he tried to fight back tears. With a shaky hand, Clement reached under his pillow and drew out a small but chunky, battered leather notebook. Philip looked down at it with confusion.

"In this notebook I have described modifications that I made to the house after the snow came. If the Tullocks try anything underhanded, the instructions in here should help you."

Philip flipped through the first few pages of the notebook. His eyes grew wide at what he saw. But apparently Clement's mind had already turned to another, even more difficult matter. His eyes flicked about in the darkness as he seemed to wrestle with something inside. When he spoke again, his voice was hesitant.

"If the sun doesn't come . . . ," he began.

"But it will!" Philip blurted. "Like you said."

"I know. But if it *doesn't* . . . ," Clement urged, ". . . look on the back of the notebook."

Philip turned the notebook over in his hand. Embedded in the thick board of the back cover was a small compartment with a brass lock, and attached by a tiny chain was a miniature key.

"If things are ever looking utterly hopeless, then unlock it and read what is written within," Clement said. Philip shook his head. What was this all about?

"But *only* if things are hopeless, I beg you," Clement went on huskily. "For if you do open it, you will *hate* me."

"Father, you don't know what you're saying. You're unwell," Philip exclaimed.

Clement gave a small, sad smile. "You won't need it anyway, for the sun will return, won't it? Make them beautifully."

Then he closed his eyes and his last breath left him. And now, sitting at his workbench, Philip rubbed the lock on the back of the notebook as though in a trance. He and Elizabeth had agreed a long time ago that he would never open it. That would be to admit defeat, to suggest the sun would never shine again, ever—and that was something a Breeze could not believe. Their lives depended on it. But did Elizabeth feel differently now? No! He threw the notebook aside suddenly and grabbed the bag of vendilium.

"The sun will return. Make them beautifully," Philip muttered to himself. He pulled some complicated-looking plans into the middle of his bench and began to work.

• • •

In the middle of the night, Rufus and Madeline crept downstairs to their father with a bowl of soup, a scrap of bread and a glass of yak's milk. He barely noticed their arrival until Madeline insisted finally, "Father, will you *please* eat and drink something!"

They watched him eat quickly in distracted gulps, his eyes roving over his workbench all the while, his fingers twitching to get back to it. Their father's skillful hands were never still that night, metal surfaces flashed in the dim candlelight, sparks flew and screws squealed into place. Madeline loved seeing her father at work like this. She rested her chin on her hand and her bright eyes followed his every move. Rufus took a more studied approach, keenly observing his father's technique and logic, then scribbling notes on neat pieces of card he always had somewhere about him. Occasionally they glanced at each other with excitement.

But later, weariness crept up on them, and eventually they settled down to sleep on the workshop steps. Their father worked on. Finally, as an insipid sun tried to penetrate the gray snow clouds of Pinrut to show morning had come again, Madeline raised her head from her brother's shoulder and her father stepped back from his workbench. His face was pale and streaked with oil, his chin heavy with blond stubble. But the machine was finished.

On the workbench before Rufus and Madeline sat an incredible thing. A line of curved and dappled beaten brass panels overlapped one another to create a long tubular shape. And several pairs of delicate brass legs held the intriguing thing upright. It resembled a large golden millipede, just like the one Rufus had pointed out to Madeline in one of her books a week before. They had never seen a real one thanks to Pinrut's uniquely frozen climate of late, but they couldn't help thinking this was far better anyway. The only marked difference in shape from the insect were the three blades attached atop either end of the paneled tube, like giant copper sycamore seeds.

Madeline squeaked with delight as she spotted the glass window that ran all the way down one side of the mechanical wonder, cleverly allowing a perfect view of the serpentine maze of ratchets, cogs and coils inside.

"It's beautiful," she breathed.

Rufus could bear it no longer. "Yes, but how does it *work*, Father?"

Philip's eyes twinkled as he began to rub his palms together rapidly, warming them. "Remember—vendilium has excellent heat-sensitive and conducting qualities." He pressed his reddened forefinger into an indentation on top of what might be considered the golden millipede's head.

Rufus had already spotted strips of vendilium metal

running like veins through this hollow . . . and now those veins began to glow.

The cogs inside the mechanical creature started to turn, ratchets clicked into action and Madeline felt a spark of excitement ignite in her stomach. It was working!

The device made an endearing puffing noise, like a mini steam engine—which Rufus realized it probably was. Next, the blades began to whirr and then, to Rufus and Madeline's amazement, the machine rippled like a wave and began to clamber quickly up their father's arm, which was resting on the workbench, and across his shoulders. Once there its legs collapsed and it draped itself around his neck, more like a bizarre scarf than any kind of insect now.

Philip raised his hands in victory and strolled around his workshop as the machine's puffing efforts became faster and more pronounced. The blades whirred on either side of his chin and fanned his hair from his face.

"Heat-activated and hands-free!" Philip exclaimed. "Go anywhere! A hot day, touch the panel with a hot hand and—instant cool air! No more sweaty necks and foreheads, eh? What do you think?"

Rufus and Madeline applauded. Then their father shivered and his face fell. He shrugged the device from his shoulders and it wafted to the floor, its still-whirring blades slowing its fall.

"Father . . . ?" Madeline said anxiously.

"Another fan to add to the others," Philip replied, and it seemed as though he were suddenly lost in a trance. "For generations, the Breeze family has made them. And every generation has come up with something better, more complex, more beautiful than the last. They're piled high in every corner of this house—new and old . . ."

Their father chewed on his lip for a moment, his eyes glazed. "And all of them utterly useless in a land of constant snow."

"But . . . ," Rufus tried.

Philip switched his gaze back to Rufus and Madeline and smiled weakly. "But the sun's coming back, right? And soon?"

Rufus and Madeline nodded desperately in unison.

"Put this one with the others upstairs. I'll be up later." Rufus put a comforting arm around his sister as, with utmost care, she carried the latest fan out of the workshop.

"I can do better, Father," Philip mumbled from behind them, and he pulled a fresh sheet of paper out and began to draw once more.

# Bartholomew Tullock the Tyrant

On a cliff overlooking Pinrut sat the Tullock mansion. It was an awe-inspiring structure with its tall windows and towers that reached high into the sky like muscular arms sporting defiant fists. The side that wasn't facing the town looked out over a churning, dark gray sea full of massive, jagged icebergs. The whole building was covered in a kind of damp mold, which gave it the appearance of a giant green beast—with snowy dandruff—hunched over the town, about to pounce.

The central tower was the tallest and straightest of them all. It seemed to point upward into the very heart of the unending snowstorm that always surrounded it. At the top of the tower, on each side, were four enormous barometer dials. As with any ordinary barometer dial, all kinds of weather conditions were depicted on those four faces, but the four metal hands pointed firmly at the same small white metal symbols that they had pointed at for years—snow. Always snow. Stone steps led from the narrow ledge that ran around the base of the barometer faces all the way down to a metal-studded door in the bottom of the tower.

On the other side of that metal-studded door, Bartholomew Tullock stared into a series of glass domes. He was a handsome man, barely a month or so older than Philip Breeze. His hair was black and fell in wavy locks around his determined brow, and his jaw was square and dark with stubble. But there was evidence of a cruel heart in the lines around his eyes and the down-turned corners of his lips. Even when he smiled, the corners of his lips did not. He was smiling now. A malevolent glee flooded through him as, thanks to several giant telescopes and some cleverly arranged mirrors, he watched the snow fall all over Pinrut in his monitoring devices. This was his weather room, and all was well as long as the domes showed the thick white flurry ever settling on the rows and rows of small Tullock-owned gray houses that he forced most Pinrutians to inhabit.

Satisfied, Tullock tapped on the decorative rug beneath his feet and turned on his heels. Today was his favorite day of the month. It was the day he made the Breeze family squirm.

He whistled to himself as he strode out of the weather room and clattered down the sweeping stone staircase that led to the cavernous main hall.

It was a shadowy, sinister room with immense pillars

and a cold, shiny floor of black-and-white marble squares. Dozens of stuffed animals stared down from the walls in various poses. Tullock tried not to look at them as he strode across the hall toward his mother, who was snoring repulsively in an armchair by the gigantic fireplace.

"I have some wonderful news, Mother," Tullock boomed.

Old Aspid Tullock awoke with a snarl.

"What is it? I was having a lovely dream about carrot cake. I was guzzling it down while people all around me were fainting with hunger."

"The snowstorm's as powerful as ever." Tullock's cold eyes glittered with triumph.

Aspid grinned maliciously. The few teeth she had left were gold, and the firelight reflected off the metal.

"How delightful, Tully," she said.

"Do you know what I love about those white flakes of joy?" Tullock asked as he spread his arms wide and spun his way into the middle of the hall.

"What?"

"The misery they cause." Tullock laughed. "How they enslave everyone to me. How they have made my business interests thrive while all others have gone under. How they have made me rich and splendid while all my workers live in gray squalor!"

His laughter faded away, to be replaced by a steely

sense of purpose. "All, that is, except the Breeze family. But they can't hold out much longer. Soon, they too will be mine."

"Show no mercy, son," Aspid said, her voice low and scratchy.

"Naturally," Tullock sneered, and he strode out of the hall.

The thick snow swirled around Rufus as he followed his mother from gray door to gray door. It was always like this shortly before Tullock came for a repayment—a tense scrabble by Mother to raise money while, Rufus made himself admit it, Father had his head in the clouds, or workshop anyway.

Tonight Elizabeth was clutching a large bundle of clothing, but so far she had sold nothing. Sometimes she found herself thinking that the blizzard would just swallow her and her family and no one would even notice.

But she would not voice such a thought aloud in front of Rufus. As she stopped at the next door, she took a deep breath, then rapped sharply on it. Rufus gave her a supportive grin. A middle-aged woman etched gray by the vestiges of grime answered the door. Despite her shabby, downtrodden appearance, Arabella smiled warmly when she saw Elizabeth on the doorstep, struggling with the weight of clothing.

"It's your presentation that always wins me over," Arabella said. "You know, it looks so irresistible tangled in a big ball like that."

"I know, I know," Elizabeth sighed. "But there's some good stuff in here." She rummaged in the woolen pile and pulled out a finely woven shawl. "This is one I just finished."

"And I think it's beautiful," Rufus said gruffly, wedging his thumbs into his toolbelt. "We Breezes pride ourselves on our superior workmanship."

"You're right, Rufus. It's lovely," Arabella said. She sighed and looked from Rufus to his mother with great weariness. "But, you know, we're really short at the moment, Elizabeth. We've barely enough to put food on the table."

"But it's Tullock day," Elizabeth whispered. Rufus tried not to hear the fear and desperation in her voice.

"All right, all right, but I can only take one of the scarves—a small one," Arabella said as she rummaged in a pocket for a few copper coins.

Elizabeth handed over a scarf and took the money.

The coins looked tiny and meager in her palm. Snowflakes landed on them instantly like ghostly vultures.

"Maybe I'll be able to buy the shawl next week," Arabella said, trying to sound bright.

"Might be too late by then," Elizabeth muttered almost under her breath. But then she looked at Arabella and smiled. "Ignore me. We'll be all right."

"Hey, Elizabeth, don't take any nonsense from that creep," Arabella called after her as she closed the door.

Elizabeth clenched the tiny coins in her fist, and as she smiled weakly at Rufus, he knew—this Tullock day was going to be the worst yet.

# Heavy Weather

To the east, Sebastian Silver and Mesmer, the blue-haired terrier of much brain, were crossing a most spectacular landscape. The bog of Pluverton had given way to lush sweeping hills with valleys full of fast-moving rivers. But vast, purple clouds still hung in the sky like vivid bruises, and the rain was almost as heavy as ever.

Sebastian squeezed the corner of his cape in a vain attempt to dry it out slightly.

"My tailor is going to be so mad with me," he said. Wooden bridges spanned the many rivers and streams around Pluverton, and Sebastian and Mesmer had been crossing them for days. Several had been scarily spindly, considering the overloaded rivers that thrashed between and against their warped legs. But now, as Sebastian and Mesmer emerged from a rain-soaked cluster of willow trees, they took in the most rickety bridge yet. It stretched out before them, hundreds of feet above the river it spanned, like a giant daddy longlegs. However, it wasn't the long, matchstick-thin legs that made Mesmer fall back onto his haunches and howl. And it wasn't the yawning gaps in the walkway that threatened to drop travelers to their doom that made Sebastian stop and gulp. No. The two companions were stunned by the thick snow blizzard that began to fall in a sheer wall exactly halfway across the bridge and valley.

Sebastian peered downward. The river nearest their side of the valley, where it was raining, was rushing along, violent and unheeded. But from what he could make out through the snowstorm, the half of the river nearest the far side of the valley was frozen solid.

"It's just like the wall of rain we walked into before reaching Pluverton last week," Sebastian said eventually. "In fact, ever since we headed north a month ago, the elements have been decidedly strange. And they're getting stranger."

Mesmer whined in agreement.

"Still, must keep moving," Sebastian continued. "Mother Nature may be on vacation, but it doesn't keep us from seeking our fortunes!"

He put a foot on the bridge and tried to ignore the extreme swaying motion and sharp protesting creaks that ensued. Mesmer's big eyes blinked behind his furry blue fringe. He didn't move.

"You old scaredy-cat!" Sebastian quavered, determinedly *not* looking down at the surging water far below.

Mesmer raised an indignant eyebrow at the insult. But he still didn't move.

"Fine! I'll have to carry you then," Sebastian snapped, and he tiptoed back off the bridge toward Mesmer, who gave a low, warning growl.

"It's fine, Mesmer. Really," Sebastian cooed. But as he reached for him, the dog took off in the opposite direction, ears flying.

"We're not going back that way," Sebastian yelled as he threw his body across Mesmer's and pulled the quivering dog tight to his chest. "We can't—remember?"

One foot at a time Sebastian edged his way across the bridge, ignoring Mesmer's plaintive yelps. As he reached the middle, he paused, took one last look about him at the rain-sodden valley, then stepped into the snow. The harsh, rhythmic drumming of raindrops was replaced suddenly with a silent caress of cold feathers.

"Well, it is exceedingly nice to be out of the rain anyway," Sebastian said as he pulled a thicker cloak from the leather satchel slung across his back. He scrunched carefully across the rest of the snow-laden bridge, stepped off the end with relief—and fell into a snowdrift up to his knees. Mesmer huffed and sniffled.

"At least, I think it is," Sebastian added.

Tullock paused outside the ornate if worn front door. He enjoyed the anticipation—that delicious moment before the fun really began. On either side of him were two members of his Hammer Squad. They wore impenetrable suits of armor made of thick burnished metal, and helmets with dark blue, bulbous glass domes where eyes could look out and a protruding mouthpiece that resembled the top of a rusting pepper shaker. Any sign of the being within was hidden. In fact, some of the Pinrut townsfolk believed that there was no being within, only the gray fog of misery. And that was just how Tullock liked it.

Both these squad members were identically dressed, therefore, except for a single large spike on one helmet where the other had three. They each hefted huge iron hammers.

"As ever, this house is your playground but you play by my rules. Understood?" Tullock muttered to his two aides. One-spike and Three-spike nodded in unison.

"Good. Your obedience to me will pay you well," Tullock said.

A little way off, Arabella leaned out from the front door of her small gray house. "Scared to go in on your own, Tullock?"

Tullock turned toward her, evil glinting like a dagger in the corner of his eye.

"Fear, my dear Arabella, is my loyal servant," Tullock said. "And unless you want a visit from that loyal servant, I suggest you go inside and lock your door."

Arabella's bravado left her rapidly, like wind deserting the sails of a galleon. She shuffled backward. A moment later the sound of a bolt being scraped back into place pierced the wintry silence. Tullock turned his attention to One-spike and gave a quick, savage nod.

SIX

# A Fearful Visit

Rufus was trying to concentrate, but it was hard with his mother pacing back and forth between his workbench and the grandfather clock by the door. It was almost time.

The rhythmic sound of sawing drifted up from the underground workshop. Rufus noticed his mother's hands were clenching in time to the noise. As he watched, her gaze flitted over the eclectic collection of fans that clicked and whirred softly in the shadows. Then she rolled her eyes and cursed silently.

Sadly, Rufus returned to his work. He pumped the lever at his foot and the large drill in his hands began to turn. He pressed forward and continued boring a hole in a triangular piece of metal clamped to the bench before him. Madeline stood next to him pouring water onto the spinning drill bit.

"That's it, Madeline. Keep it cool or it'll break," Rufus yelled above the noise of the instrument.

"I know, Ru! I'm not a frosthead," Madeline replied. The sudden hammering on the door made them all jump. The color drained from their mother's face in an instant. Rufus and Madeline let the drill whine to a halt.

The hammering came again. The few remaining china plates on the dresser rattled.

"Upstairs, you two. Now," Elizabeth urged.

Rufus drew himself up as tall as he could. "We want to stay."

"You shouldn't face that snow-dome alone," Madeline added. "Please."

Their mother's voice was firm. "Go to your rooms." Dragging their heels, Rufus and Madeline thudded reluctantly up the stairs. But as their mother headed for the door, they turned quickly and crouched on the landing to listen as she slid back the bolt.

Tullock glided into the house, One-spike and Three-spike following close behind. He wore a long bloodred coat with white buttons shaped like snowflakes, and the hem of the garment swished luxuriously around his black leather-booted ankles.

"Good evening, Lizzie. Looking lovely as always," Tullock boomed.

"My name's Elizabeth."

"You tell him, Mother," Madeline muttered as Rufus put a finger to his lips to remind his sister to keep quiet. Tullock moved closer to Elizabeth. With an idle motion he twirled a lock of her hair in his fingers. Rufus felt an uneasy flicker of fear in his stomach.

"Pay back all the money you owe me and I'll call you Rosebud," Tullock went on.

Elizabeth pulled away from him with a look of disdain.

"Elizabeth *Breeze*," she said.

"Sometimes I weep when I think about that fact," Tullock answered, and Madeline thought he did sound almost . . . sad. But the soft tone was gone again so quickly she wasn't sure she hadn't imagined it.

"Where is Windy? Hmm?" Tullock snapped now. "Windy! Come out here!"

Madeline flinched at the sneer in Tullock's bellow. Rufus peered down the stairs.

"If Father doesn't come up, I'm going down," he whispered fiercely. "Mother shouldn't be alone with that utter ice cube, and . . . I am the other man of the house."

Madeline grabbed Rufus's arm. "But I don't want Father to come up and get cross. He's got no chance against Tullock and his two tin-heads," she said.

"He should at least try."

Down below, Philip's workshop was full of steam—the result of the piston saw, which was currently hacking its way through several thick strips of steel. Beads of sweat stood out on Philip's forehead and his eyes shone. This was going to be his most amazing fan yet. He knew it. But darkness suddenly clouded Philip's pleasant daydreams.

A familiar voice was seeping through the floorboards from above. A harsh, grating tone that had the force to make itself heard over a steam-powered piston saw.

Tullock.

With a bad-tempered grunt, Philip flipped the pressure-release valve on the saw and it fell silent with a hiss and a high-pitched whistle. He bounded up the steps and threw the wooden trapdoor open.

"He's come up," Rufus said, his eyes gleaming. He couldn't see his father, but he had heard the trapdoor crash open and he *could* see the clouds of steam that were now billowing up from the workshop.

"Oh, I wish he hadn't," Madeline said.

"There you are, Windy!" Tullock gloated as the air cleared. "You owe me some money." Tullock held out a smooth, pale hand.

Philip paced over to stare down at it. "What an irritatingly long life line you have," he remarked.

Their mother winced, but up on the landing Rufus and Madeline couldn't help but smirk at each other. Tullock scowled. He was taller than Philip and now he pushed back his shoulders to emphasize the fact.

"Let's not tarry in the blizzard, Windy," he barked. "Just pay me what you owe me this month or you know what happens."

"This is *our* house!" Philip cried.

Tullock groaned. "Every month it's the same." He leaned in close to Philip, his black eyes wide and glaring. "Get this into your overheated head: unless you give me my monthly four gold coins as agreed with your father, this is *my* house, and if I so wished, I could have it flattened immediately." His eyes flicked to Elizabeth for barely a moment. "It's only out of the goodness of my heart that I let you carry on living here when payments are consistently late or made up of tatty pieces of furniture. Now for the last time, where's my frosting money!"

Elizabeth strode to the dresser and took down a small bag. She handed it to Tullock.

"Much obliged," he said as he weighed the bag in his hand. "You're short."

"We can give you the rest next week," Elizabeth tried. Rufus and Madeline exchanged glances. They could feel the tension building in the room, spreading up the stairs to where they were crouched on the landing. And what their father said next did not look set to help matters.

"When the sun comes and we are debt-free, I shall enjoy watching you sweat!"

Tullock rocked back on his heels and allowed himself a small smile of satisfaction. "The sun will never return. Trust me."

"You're wrong. It will be here soon," Philip said. "It has to be, after so long."

At the top of the stairs Rufus looked at Madeline. "It *will* be here soon," he whispered and she nodded. But somehow neither of them felt as sure as they wanted to. Not anymore.

They watched Tullock move closer to their mother, lowering his voice to a conspiratorial whisper as he gazed over her shoulder at the machines twinkling in the darkness.

Madeline had to force her head between the banisters to get near enough to hear.

"You're *still* short. I'll take the contraptions in payment." Tullock leaned closer still to Elizabeth and breathed in deeply, his nostrils flaring. "I collect beautiful things."

"Get away from my wife!" Philip barked. "My father would never have given them to you and neither will I!"

Tullock squinted at Philip witheringly. "Your father . . ." His lip curled. "Oh yes . . . a man of fine principles."

"He was!" Philip snapped defiantly, though he felt strangely unnerved by Tullock's knowing tone.

Tullock nodded in exaggerated agreement with Philip. Then his brow furrowed once more. He slapped his hands together making a sharp *crack*.

"So if not the machines, what are you offering me, man?"

"How about I let you leave here in one piece?" Philip ventured.

One-spike and Three-spike both took a threatening

step forward. Madeline held her breath as her father clenched his fists and readied himself.

"Take the clock," Elizabeth blurted suddenly. "It belonged to my great-aunt. It's valuable."

Madeline saw her father turn to her mother in shock, but Elizabeth avoided his gaze.

"Why, thank you. It's a handsome piece," Tullock was saying. He ran his fingers over the polished wood, then gave a nod to Three-spike. "Smash it."

And with an almighty swing of his hammer Three-spike shattered it into tiny pieces. Splinters, springs and cogs flew through the air and clattered to the floor.

Their mother gasped, her long pale fingers shooting up to cover her face, and Madeline had to act fast to keep Rufus from dashing down the stairs to her. With all her strength Madeline clung to him while still managing to chew on the nail of her little finger in an earnest attempt not to cry.

But there was nothing she could do from up there to stop her father. He gave an outraged roar and launched himself at Tullock. One-spike reacted with alarming speed. Within seconds Philip's arms were pinned by his sides and One-spike had him in a headlock. It was only the finger in her mouth that prevented Madeline from yelping.

Tullock plucked a stray splinter from his immaculate woolen coat and flicked it onto the floor with disdain.

"My patience is wearing thin. Short-change me again and the whole house gets the hammer." He sidled up to the squirming Philip. "You know where you should be right now? Working in my fields, living in one of my gray shacks—like my other . . . employees. In the long run it's the only way your family will survive."

Madeline watched her father look sadly at her mother before he dropped his gaze to the floor, his teeth clenched. She gulped. Surely that wasn't what her mother wanted. Things hadn't got *that* bad . . . had they?

Tullock glanced at the remains of the clock. "Ooh! Is that the time? Better be off." He turned toward the stairs. "You may come down now, dear sweet little Breezes! The nasty man is leaving."

He strode to the door, then turned back, making sure Elizabeth had the benefit of his best side.

"Think about me," he said, his voice deliberately warm and smooth.

"Go home to your mother," Elizabeth retorted.

Tullock seemed to shrink a little. He paused. But eventually he walked back out into the blizzard without saying another word.

One-spike threw Philip to the floor and fell into step with Three-spike, marching after their master.

Philip clambered to his feet and staggered to the door.

"You're adrift, Tullock!" he yelled. "Adrift in a dark place!"

But Tullock and his two sinister henchmen were already gone, swallowed up by the eternal snowstorm.

Philip collapsed against the door frame—all energy spent. Elizabeth wrapped her arms around him.

"Oh, Philip, what will it take for you to see sense?" she said. "Your father wouldn't have wanted this."

"You're wrong, Lizzie," Philip muttered. "I can hear my father cheering me on."

Rufus and Madeline tiptoed down the stairs and watched their mother and father clinging to each other. If ever the Breeze family needed help, it was now.

SEVEN

# Sebastian and Mesmer Wrestle with the Elements

The blizzard licked at Sebastian Silver and Mesmer with a million icy tongues as they made their way, slipping and sliding, along a towering ridge of ice. It was as though a river had been blown from its bed then frozen instantly into a long, irregular wall. Sebastian had clambered up onto it, thinking progress there would be quicker and safer than struggling through the thick drifts that lay on either side. But now, as he and Mesmer slithered and skidded along, he wasn't so sure.

Behind him, Mesmer whined as his frozen paws fought for traction. Sebastian looked down and took an inventory of all the bizarre items encased in the ice below them. There were small boats and fishing rods and sunhats and deck chairs. A summer's day thrown into the air, then frozen there.

"Where *are* we, Mesmer?" Sebastian asked.

A muted—and slightly dismayed—yelp made Sebastian spin around, then slide, then slip, then regain his balance at last. Mesmer was no longer there.

"Where are *you*, Mesmer?" Sebastian called before he spotted a dog-shaped hole in a snowdrift below and dropped down off the icy wall instantly. The snow was so deep it took Sebastian a couple of minutes to dig his way through to the buried blue-haired terrier.

When he finally pulled him out, Mesmer was rigid, completely surrounded by a thin layer of ice. It took even longer for Sebastian to chip all the ice away—he'd used his travel ice pick to chop ice for the odd evening cocktail in the past, but freeing a distinctly petrified-looking dog took a little more care. Still, Mesmer was finally freed.

"Need to get you somewhere warm, and quick," Sebastian said, bundling the dog up in his coat and holding him to his chest.

He battled gamely on up a sharp rise and at last looked down into the valley beyond. The dim lights of a town were just visible through the gray, swirling maelstrom.

"Now, which is the quickest way down?" Sebastian mused as he observed the steep, tree-lined mountain slope that fell away beneath him. "Got to be this way, methinks."

Mesmer let out a weak, warning yap.

"It's all right," Sebastian chuckled reassuringly. "You know I'm big on shortcuts."

The blue-haired terrier's eyebrows rose up his furry face, all the way to his ears.

Sebastian stepped confidently around a fir tree, tripped over the sleeve of his coat, which was dangling from Mesmer's chilled body, and found himself hurtling downhill on his backside between the trees, skidding on hard, compacted snow.

"Woooooooaaaahh!" Sebastian cried.

"Yoooooowwlll!" Mesmer howled.

A colony of hobo penguins scattered in all directions as the noisy travelers bumped and sped their way down the mountain. A shocked snow fox ducked into its den. But fortune often favors the brave and foolhardy, and so it was with Sebastian and Mesmer. Instead of ending up splattered thinly over one of the fir trees, like jam on bread, they rumbled unharmed all the way to the bottom of the mountain.

Sebastian shook himself free of snow and let out a long, verging on the hysterical, laugh. "Now, that's the only way to travel!" he said. "Let's do it again."

Mesmer gave a bad-tempered growl.

"'PINRUT—we may be backward but it's a living. Population 982. Twinned with Torrac,'" Sebastian read aloud. "Never mind Torrac. Right now I'd like to be twinned with a warm bed."

They pushed on into Pinrut as night fell, and what a

strange place it seemed. Rows of gray, uniform houses, with small windows, lined twisting, snow-covered streets. The rooftops seemed to be nothing more than rusting sheets of metal buckling under the weight of snow. From a few windows, cool blue candlelight flickered, as though fire itself had lost the power to be warm and bright in this place.

Mesmer gave a sudden horrified howl and jumped up into his friend's arms. Sebastian followed his wild gaze and took in a frozen cat leaping toward an equally frozen seagull, the two of them joined by a glittering column of ice, like a macabre statue.

"You know, if I weren't frozen already, I would find this place quite chilling," Sebastian said in hushed tones.

They walked on.

"Do you think anyone will take us in?" he added hopelessly. "It doesn't look very . . . friendly."

But as they turned a corner, the street gave way to an open area, and in the middle of this was the most exquisite and unusual house Sebastian had ever seen. The windows were made up of segments of glass like slices from a cake. The walls seemed similarly constructed, though in wood. They reminded Sebastian of something, but he couldn't think what. The snow-laden roof was a higgledy-piggledy mixture of angles and corners, a bit like a load of playing cards leaning up against one another, and the door, though worn, was a dark wood delight with curving brass hinges and a stunning sun motif carved into it. Admittedly the icicled veranda, with decorative wooden posts and a swing seat, seemed strangely incongruous, given the climate. Sebastian couldn't imagine anyone huddling there to watch the snow fall. But the ornate if battered lamps that hung from its eaves gave off a welcoming glow. It was a pleasingly solid house, full of character and charm, and it lifted the spirits after row upon row of the nondescript gray dwellings.

"That looks like our kind of place!" Sebastian exclaimed.

EIGHT

# Dream Machines

Elizabeth was doing her best to pick up the hundreds of clock parts that lay scattered across the floor. She shuffled about on her knees, sweeping them into a dustpan. Madeline watched her father as he peered into what was left of the mechanism. She knew his mind would be mapping the remains, calculating whether the parts could be put back together in harmony once more.

"I can fix it," he said eventually.

Elizabeth looked up at Philip with a sheen of sadness in her green eyes. "Can you?" she said, and Rufus knew she wasn't talking about the clock.

Desperate, he cast around for something to cheer them all up, or at least distract them from their worries. Suddenly, he dashed into the shadows beneath the stairs, then emerged holding one of his father's fans. Madeline grinned as he put it down on the dining table and she realized what he was up to.

"That's one of my favorites too," she said.

The main body of the machine was made of a sky-blue metal. A yellow ovoid at one end gave the appearance of a head, and two large red crystals resembled staring eyes while two little leather flaps looked like ears. At the other end was a long leather "tail" laced through with little red-brown feathers. Four thin copper legs with hinges and springs supported the whole thing. The effect was that of a small clockwork monkey leaning forward on all fours.

"Ready?" Rufus asked with a glint in his eyes. Madeline nodded and nibbled at the nail on her little finger with delight.

Elizabeth looked up from her sweeping and groaned.

"Rufus, can you *not* do that now?" she said.

"But Mother, this one is funny," Rufus said. And with that he snapped the tail sharply. The energy cracked along the tail in a pulsing wave and the two red eyes lit up. In the next instant the legs began to pump and the machine leaped from the table and scurried across the floor, flicking clock parts everywhere.

Their mother glowered. But Rufus and Madeline were following the progress of the machine with impish grins.

It scaled a wall at speed and then, as it reached the top, launched itself into thin air. But as it plummeted toward the floor, the tail began to whirr—slowly at first, then faster and faster, until it was nothing but a blur. Madeline laughed as the mischievous machine's descent slowed until it was brought to a complete halt—it hung in midair now, its spinning tail keeping it suspended. Her father moved closer to it. His blond hair ruffled up as the draft generated by the hovering fan reached him. Rufus and Madeline exchanged relieved looks as a smile spread across his face once more.

Their mother stood up. She couldn't help but smile too. It had been a long time since she had seen her family looking so together and happy.

Then there was a sharp knock at the door. Smiles forgotten, they all spun to look in its direction. The whirring leather tail hit Philip sharply in the back of the head and the monkey machine clattered to the floor and fell silent.

"I wonder who that can be," Philip said, rubbing his head.

"What if that snow-dome's come back?" Madeline asked with wide eyes.

She felt her mother draw her close, and Rufus stepped protectively in front of them both as Philip reached for the bolt.

"Don't open it, Father," Madeline blurted. She chewed at the nail on her little finger again until her mother gently pushed her hand away from her mouth.

"We open the door and behave in a dignified fashion," Elizabeth said. "We'll give him no reason to come through it with force."

Philip nodded his agreement and drew back the bolt. But as he cautiously opened the door, he was greeted not by a fuming Tullock but by a grubby-looking man in a yellow cape and hat, with an icicle hanging from his nose.

"My name is S-Sebastian S-Silver," the man chattered through purple lips. "You don't have to invite me in, but p-p-p-please take my dog. His fur is meant to be blue but not, I b-believe, his tongue."

At this moment Mesmer let out a violent sneeze.

Rufus felt a wave of relief wash over him. His mother dashed forward from behind him. "Please do come in. Both of you."

"You look frozen stiff," Madeline added.

Sebastian stepped inside, removed his hat and spread his arms wide.

"Ah! W-warmth! D-dryness! A haven from the strangely er-er-erratic elements!"

The icicle dropped from his nose and impaled him in the foot.

"Argh!" He doubled over quickly and plucked the sharp, icy point from his boot. "Don't worry! This item of footwear is made of exceptionally good quality, thick leather—sold a consignment of them not a month ago.

I can say with absolute confidence that my boot is probably not filling up with blood. Magnificoco!"

Rufus and Madeline exchanged a questioning look.

"I have a spare pair if anyone's interested in buying, actually . . . no . . . ?"

With a despairing glance at his still-gabbling master Mesmer padded over to the monkey-shaped machine that lay inert on the floor. He sniffed it, then pawed at it cautiously. The leather tail gave a quick flick and Mesmer jumped back with a suspicious growl. Sebastian's interest was sparked immediately. And now he noticed the other startling machines piled on every spare surface and in every nook and cranny of the room. He raised his eyebrows in surprise.

"Dream machines, Mesmer," he said as he pulled a magnifying glass from his pocket and leaned to examine the device closest to him. "Exquisite . . ."

"Want to buy one?" said Madeline brashly.

"Madeline!" her mother admonished.

But Sebastian spun around and pointed a finger at Madeline. "I'd like to buy them all," he declared. "But unfortunately, at this particular moment, due to unforeseen circumstances, I don't have a penny to my name . . ." Sebastian flushed, then cleared his throat. "I do have one question though. What *are* they?"

Philip frowned. "They're fans, of course. Machines to cool you when you're hot." He hooked his thumbs into his toolbelt and lifted his chin with more than a hint of pride. "You are looking at Philip Breeze, the fanmaker of Pinrut. The latest in a long line of true, innovative artists."

Sebastian glanced toward the windows. "Of course!" he said. "Old-fashioned handheld fans! That's what your windows and wall panels reminded me of."

"We've come a long way since those, haven't we, Father?" Rufus said proudly, but Sebastian wasn't listening.

"The fanmaker of *frozen* Pinrut . . . ," he was mumbling to himself, nodding slowly. "But Mr. Breeze, I hadn't realized."

"What?" Philip asked.

Sebastian bounded over to him and shook him vigorously by the hand. "Why, you're completely mad!"

NINE

# The Bloodcurdling Scratskin

The carriage emerged from the wood at great speed. It looked like a giant beetle—gloss black and covered in sharp spikes. Four muscular midnight stallions hauled it, their mouths frothing at the bit and their long manes streaming back as far as their tails. Their eyes were wild. A shadowy, stick-thin figure sitting atop the carriage lashed at the charging beasts with no mercy.

Inside, Tullock sat alone, reflecting on the evening's events. They had been most enjoyable, though upsetting Elizabeth had been verging on the regrettable. Still, she deserved all she got for now, for throwing her lot in with such a deranged imbecile.

The impressively revolting Tullock mansion lay up ahead on the edge of the cliff, shrouded in swirling eddies of snow. Tullock watched his hulking abode loom into view with an all-consuming pride.

"Home sweet home," he murmured to himself. Suddenly the carriage lurched as it hit a rock. Tullock leaned from the window and gulped as he saw how close the carriage wheels were to the cliff edge. He shouted up to the driver. "Scratskin, have more care!"

Scratskin plucked a flaming torch from the seat beside him and turned his square bony shoulders so he was looking back at Tullock. The torch held high lit Scratskin from behind so all Tullock could see was a skeletal silhouette. But then Scratskin moved the light under his chin to reveal his terrible, gaunt visage. Bulging eyes with no apparent eyelids stared out from bone-white skin. Massive gums protruded from his almost lipless mouth boasting only six tiny yellow stumps of teeth. He flared his pinched nostrils and spoke with a voice like iron chains being dragged over gravel. "Do *you* want to drive?"

Tullock recoiled and fought the urge to gag. He shook his head vehemently. Then, in an attempt to hide his momentary loss of composure, he just managed to call out, "No, I'm very comfortable here, thank you, Scratskin," before ducking back inside the carriage. He was the master. So why did Scratskin make him feel like his orders were actually suggestions to be ignored at will? He peered at the seat in front of him. It was covered in feathers and fur and liberal helpings of sawdust. Clearly, on top of everything else, Scratskin was using the Tullock family carriage for his own questionable errands.

The carriage skidded to a halt in front of the main

doors. Tullock barely had time to get out before it raced off again toward the stables.

"And give it a clean!" Tullock yelled after the departing vehicle. "It's like a parrot cage in there!" Feeling less than cherished by his workers, Tullock ignored the six Hammer Squad members that lined the wide path to his monstrous front door and strode inside.

Tullock stormed into the main hall still reflecting on the Breezes. Oh, how he wanted to demolish their horribly charming house, squash it into the ground and dance on the remains. But Elizabeth made things complicated. One day she would be his. She could not resist his charm, good looks and awe-inspiring wealth for much longer, surely, so for now he would not do anything that might push her away forever. Besides, annoyingly, she did keep coming through with the payments somehow. But when they ran out of things to sell, were starving to death . . . then his time would come, to break smug Philip Breeze in his fields and to reveal to Elizabeth what a pathetic man her husband really was.

Tullock leaned against the massive black marble mantelpiece and tried to ignore the new stuffed wolf on top of it, a stuffed penguin cowering before its polished fangs. The grisly results of Scratskin's taxidermy were getting everywhere! He really must have a strict word with him about it. At some point. Maybe. Tullock's mother watched him from her chair at the other end of the fireplace. She was cracking walnuts in her armpit and gobbling them noisily.

"What's eating you?" she snarled, spraying small pieces of nut over the scratchy black lace of her dress.

"The blasted Breeze family," Tullock replied. "In their fancy house being all artistic. It's nauseating. And don't get me started on him. Why is he so stubborn—and being a fanmaker? Hmm? I mean, what's the point? He's just trying to stir up a storm, start trouble. It's a good thing no one in Pinrut listens to him."

"Don't waste your time on those oddballs," Aspid mumbled, trying to suppress a belch and failing. "Let's do something exciting. How about a mystery feast? Let's get a big table and pile it high with pies filled with all manner of surprises!" Aspid started to drool. "We could invite the field workers . . . to watch"—she cackled, wiping at her chin—"their stomachs rumbling . . . as we gorge!"

"Yes, not the classiest of evenings, is it?" Tullock replied testily. He winced as his mother placed another walnut in her armpit. "Mother, must you do that? Where are the gold nutcrackers I gave you?"

"Ah, leave me alone. I like it this way. Keeps me fit." Aspid bit down on the walnut, but then spat it across the fireplace, where it landed in the mouth of a startled-looking stuffed squirrel. "Ugh, that was a bad one."

Tullock sighed and walked into the middle of the vast room. His boots clicked on the floor and he looked down to see his brooding features reflected in the dirty marble, distorted and dull.

"A real woman's touch—that's just what this place needs." He looked askance at his mother. "One day Elizabeth will be with me," he went on. "Then I shall have it all."

Aspid scowled. "Your father didn't do all this yearning and browbeating. He would have pulled himself together, rolled up his sleeves and got busy with the pastry," she said.

"Could you stop with your frankly rather unsettling 'mystery pies'!" Tullock snapped.

Aspid sucked in her cheeks and went back to cracking her nuts.

# A Cruel Punishment

Elizabeth cleared away the still half-full soup dishes while Sebastian stared at the curious contraption on the table in front of him, food forgotten. Mesmer stood upright with his front paws on the edge of the table, sniffing at the machine. It was a sphere made up of several very thin nut-brown and apple-green enameled metal panels. The whole thing rested on a ball joint and gave off a faint rustling noise like leaves being buffeted by a gentle wind. Mesmer snorted at it, and the machine undulated like a jellyfish and gave a few metallic clicks before it resumed its quiet rustling.

Mesmer dropped his chin onto the table with a confused look on his furry face. Madeline laughed and scratched behind his ears.

"Philip, these really are incredible," Sebastian said. "How does this one work?"

"Actually I have a slightly sore throat after yelling at,

er, someone earlier," Philip replied. "Rufus, do you want to . . . ?"

"Brace yourselves," Rufus said as he drew in a mighty breath. "COOL ME!" he yelled at the machine. And all of the panels on the sphere began to oscillate.

Sebastian raised his eyebrows and tried to ignore the ringing in his ears.

"Er, that's how you power it up, so to speak," Rufus explained, a little red in the face.

In the next moment the machine sprang to life. It suddenly seemed to turn itself inside out as at least twenty shimmering metal paddles shot outward on hinged arms and began to flap up and down. The whole device revolved on its ball joint. Cool air wafted from it in all directions, and everyone at the table felt a sudden chill. Sebastian shivered.

"Works well," he said, wrapping his arms around himself and clenching his jaw to stop his teeth from chattering. Mesmer dropped to the floor and took shelter under the table.

"Stop!" Madeline instructed, and with a clatter and a whisper the machine folded up on itself and became a sphere once more.

"Not much call for it tonight," Philip admitted. "Or indeed any night for a long time."

Rufus and Madeline exchanged glances. The note of

hopelessness in their father's voice had been unusual until recently, and Madeline didn't like it. Without his blind optimism and passion, what were the Breezes left with?

"But the Breeze factory mustn't let up," her mother added as she sat back down.

Sebastian ignored the jagged look that shot between her and Philip. "Accuse me of conjecture but I would surmise that when the snow came, the fan business folded?" he asked instead.

"Everything changed," Philip replied sadly.

"But why did this vile snowstorm settle its ashen heart here?" Sebastian wondered aloud.

"No one knew why," Philip answered. "We've never known."

"And besides, people were so numb with cold, they didn't care," Elizabeth added. "Liberty froze." And her stern expression softened into sympathy as she took her husband's hand. He squeezed it gratefully. Madeline kicked Rufus under the table gleefully—she definitely preferred it when her parents were like this with each other. But Rufus only frowned—much as he loved his sister, she could be so naive sometimes. He knew it wouldn't last; how could it when things had gotten so bad?

"This was once a hot region, would you believe," their father was saying now. "Families, friends and neighbors would work together and play together all the time. But when the sun was covered by these unending snow clouds, many businesses began to go under, food was scarce, money scarcer. Only the Tullocks were prepared to deal with it. They were always rich but, as luck would have it, the crops they'd planted only six months before on their extensive lands just happened to *flourish* in cold, snowy, darkened conditions . . . turnips and parsnips!"

"Revolting!" Madeline interjected, poking her tongue out. "And they're virtually all we have to eat—day in, day out."

"Ah, yes." Sebastian tried not to wrinkle his nose at the memory of the soup earlier—but it did explain its bland, watery taste.

"Soon almost everyone was working for the Tullocks," Mrs. Breeze went on. "It was the only way to put food on the table—even then only just. And when old Tullock died soon after and Bartholomew took over, he moved all his workers into the horrible gray hovels you see outside and knocked everything else down. The Tullocks own virtually the whole of Pinrut by now, and that's just the way they want it. They, along with the never-ending snow that falls forever outside our window, have broken the spirit of this town—there's . . . there's nothing good left anymore."

"We're trying to stay true to the old ideals though," Philip said quickly.

"Yes. Somehow we scrape by . . . so far," Elizabeth whispered.

"Don't worry, Mother. The sun will return!" Rufus wanted to say, desperate to cheer her up, but he found he couldn't do it.

"And when the sun comes back, we'll be ready for it!" Madeline exclaimed instead. "The people of Pinrut will turn to us when they're so hot they can barely move, won't they, Father?"

"You seem very certain," Sebastian said. "The whole snow, ice, freezing thing looked perniciously permanent to me."

"Well, the thaw's coming," Philip said, though a little halfheartedly.

Sebastian let his shrewd gaze drift to the polished fans of all shapes and sizes piled high around the room. They stood in stark contrast to the shabby surroundings—and the appearance of the Breeze family themselves.

"Meanwhile, what if the prodigious and stupendous Sebastian Silver—salesman extraordinaire—could help you shift all these fans?" Sebastian asked.

Tullock was in his study—an extravagant but gloomy room—trying to add up his income for the month. It would be enormous; it always was. A harsh rap on his study door made him jump.

"What is it?" Tullock barked.

One-spike and Three-spike clanged into the room with a thin, grubby man dressed in rags held up between them. The man was nothing more than a frightened shadow, his narrow chest heaving with torment. A copper sun pendant on a leather thong hung hopefully around his scrawny neck.

"We caught this wretch trying to break into the sunflower vault," One-spike said in a voice that sounded like it came from the bottom of a deep well.

Tullock shot to his feet and slammed two fists down on the desk in front of him. "How dare you, you vermin!" he bellowed.

"But my wife has the Pinrutian flu," the man wheezed. "Only sunflower tonic can help her."

"There are barely enough sunflowers in that vault to make tonic for me and my mother," Tullock snapped. "Never mind for your insignificant wife!"

"The vault is full and you don't even have the flu," the man retorted. He wriggled uncomfortably, but his arms seemed like twigs in the clutches of the robust Hammer Squad members.

"I don't have the flu *yet*. But some disgusting cockroach like you is probably going to inflict it on me someday!"

Tullock sat down again and plucked an embroidered handkerchief from his pocket. He clutched it to his mouth.

"Take him away," he mumbled through the cloth. "Go west and cast him onto the Great Glacier."

"No!" shrieked the man. "Please! No! Nobody can survive out there. Have mercy! My wife is ill and the rest of my family—"

But One-spike and Three-spike had already whisked the protesting Pinrutian out of the door.

Tullock lowered his handkerchief to reveal an expression of disgust. How he disliked the people who lived in his town. Especially those who had the audacity to whine and complain to him. It was only right that they should be banished to a place that spawned a million frozen nightmares.

ELEVEN

# A Map Full of Promise

Sebastian rummaged in his roomy leather satchel and, with a triumphant cry, pulled out a tatty piece of paper.

"You do realize snow doesn't cover the whole world, of course?" he said. "Or even the whole of this region?"

"Well, I . . . ," Rufus's father began.

Rufus felt faintly embarrassed. He too had always assumed the terrible unending snow was falling everywhere. They all had. Why wouldn't it be?

"Tullock told us it did," Madeline said indignantly.

"It certainly stretches a long way," Sebastian said. "Mesmer and I have the chapped lips to prove it. Then farther out east it's raining like you wouldn't believe. Awash they are. And I've heard there are storms with hailstones the size of plums to the north. But this exquisite map, which I bought at great expense from a renowned cartographer, because I only deal in the best, you understand, shows a huge area of desert immediately to the west of here."

"So it would be really hot out there?" Philip asked excitedly.

"Boiling, scorching, sweltering. Apparently even the scorpions have parasols," Sebastian answered. He spread out his hands. "Let me tell you, I have traveled the wide world, walked hand in hand with the usual seasons, sun, wind, rain and snow, but I have never seen Captain Climate on such an outlandish rampage as he is around these parts—so let's make it work for us!" He jabbed at the map. "There's one town, called Tresedira, in the middle of this desert. We'll take your fans and cooling doobries there and make you rich! Buy your life back from this tyrant Tullock."

Madeline had been watching her father all through this speech, and she smiled when she saw a joyful light in his eyes.

But Rufus was frowning at Sebastian. "Who exactly *are* you?" he asked.

"I'm a purveyor of dreams, a merchant of miracles. I'm the man to have in your corner," Sebastian replied. "And I'm only asking twenty percent of your profits."

Elizabeth, like her son, was suspicious. At this final statement she pursed her lips.

Sebastian shrewdly took in the mixed emotions in the room. He settled back in his seat and rested his feet on the sleeping Mesmer.

"It was just an idea," he went on, his eyes wide with innocence. "You four talk about it."

The persistent snowstorm was worse at night. Its feathery fingers pawed at the windows of the Breeze house and tried to find gaps and holes through which to send its insidious chill.

In a small guest room, decorated with sun-motif wallpaper, Sebastian slumbered fitfully. Mesmer lay wrapped around his feet, also adrift in the land of dreams.

"I assure you, sir, that most definitely is the rum you ordered . . . What do you mean, vinegary . . . ," Sebastian muttered between shallow snores. "Of course I'll return . . . Pluverton . . . tools. Don't you trust me? Hmm?" He turned over in his sleep, still mumbling. "What can go wrong this time? . . . I'm a merchant of miracles . . . make our fortune along with the fanmaker, I'm sure of it . . ."

Downstairs, Rufus and Madeline worked in studious silence. They often crept down to do so late at night, when their parents were asleep.

At last they were fitting together the final pieces of their first very own complete fan. It had been the labor of six months, and their fingers shook with excitement as they attached the last part.

Though not as ornate and complicated as their father's machines, it had an appealing, quirky elegance. The upright cylinder made of polished metal had a number of glass jars full of different-colored liquids strapped neatly around it. In the low light of the room the colors shimmered slickly. Tubes led from the jars, joined up, then ran into the cylinder.

Madeline poured water into the top of the device. "I think Father will decide to go west with Mr. Silver."

"If he does, he shouldn't go alone," Rufus said as he carefully opened the valves built into each of the tubes. The colored liquids started to flow toward the cylinder, meeting on the way and swirling together like a watery rainbow. "Father is brilliant when he's working, but hopeless the rest of the time, and I'm not sure I trust this Mr. Silver."

"He certainly likes the sound of his own voice—but I'd like to go anyway," Madeline said. "It'd be an amazing adventure. Besides, think of what it could mean to us and to Father!"

Rufus nodded. The machine made a peculiar gurgling noise, and a wisp of gray smoke puffed from the top. Rufus glanced at his younger sister, marveling again at how different they were from each other. She seemed almost excited at the prospect of such a trip, while all he could think about was its obstacles and how to preempt them. Wouldn't he be the more sensible choice to go, therefore, no matter how brave she was?

"You'd definitely have to stay here, Ru," Madeline said suddenly as though reading her brother's thoughts, "to protect the house—you'd be much better at sorting that out than me, plus you're bigger and stronger if Mother needs defending from that snow-dome, Tullock."

Their machine made a sudden whooshing noise, then fell silent. They looked at each other with trepidation. Had it worked? Rufus reached down into the cylinder and plucked out a ring of solid ice and slid it onto his arm. As the frozen water pressed against his flesh, he shivered and beamed from ear to ear. Madeline pulled another ring out and slipped it onto her own wrist.

"It's not strictly a fan," she said. "But we did it. It works—it *cools*."

"It was your idea," Rufus said generously.

"But you figured out how to do it," Madeline reminded him. "Do you think Father will approve?"

"Of course," Rufus said. "With my plans and your ideas we make a good team." Then his smile faded. "Promise me you'll be careful out there."

"Promise," Madeline agreed solemnly. She was determined to live up to her steadfast brother's expectations.

And with that they shook hands, their ice bracelets jangling.

Philip climbed the narrow stairs into a small study at the top of the house. He couldn't sleep. He pulled a lever and a gabled section of the roof began to extend out—its workings clunking somewhere deep within the house walls—and then fold inward on itself to make a balcony, open to the skies. Fifty small fans built into the beams above pointed upward and outward and started to whirr, creating a domed barrier of wind against the snow. Another of Clement Breeze's clever additions.

Philip stepped onto the balcony and clutched his coat tightly around him. He took in the uniform, gray houses huddled below and the hulking mass of the Tullock mansion above, just visible as a dark green imprint in the sky beyond the Reffinock forest to the south.

Philip looked over to the west and clenched his craftsman's fingers into fists. He knew what lay out there just beyond the town gates: the place where all the townspeople worked now. Perhaps he should have joined them. For his family. But if he had, how long before Rufus and Madeline, Elizabeth too, were in the fields also? Their spirits crushed . . . and fanmaking lost to the Pinrutian Breezes forever, even once the sun came back.

Yet he had to do something—he saw it in his wife's eyes. And Sebastian Silver had to be the answer. Joyfully, Philip imagined sweeping dunes full of hot, flushed, sweaty people.

As long as his family stayed safely in the house the whole time he was away, the defenses his father built should keep Tullock out and the Breeze house protected.

Hopefully. But what if they didn't? He felt a chill of fear. What if . . . ?

Philip pulled his father's notebook from a pocket and rubbed the lock again. His father's words echoed in his ears. Maybe the time had come after all . . .

Suddenly Philip sensed a presence and turned. It was Madeline, her fair hair straggly, her forehead and shabby clothes smudged with oil and her thumbs wedged into her toolbelt. He felt a sudden wave of love for his fan-making daughter.

"Father, I want to come with you to Tresedira," she said firmly.

TWELVE

# A Golden Chariot

The light of morning did little to lift the ponderous gloom that hung over Pinrut. The snow fell thickly and swirled in the air like ash. Rufus and Madeline were helping their parents heave all the fans outside—they looked strangely incongruous as the snow settled on their shining surfaces.

A black-and-white penguin fan went into action atop the pile. With its green eyes and yellow funnel for a mouth it looked just like a penguin, and its black leather flippers slapped together comically, sending out ripples of cold air.

"That one's activated by a rise in ambient light like when the sun comes out from behind a cloud. Bringing it outside must have set it off," Philip explained. An older, more traditional fan made of silk and lace, stretched over a bamboo frame, got half caught at the base of the penguin machine and unfolded, giving the more modern device a beautiful, shimmering tail. "Can somebody turn off the master switch?"

Madeline flicked it and the fan stopped abruptly.

Stacked together, the Breeze fans made an impressive sight, their colorful angled surfaces and textured curves catching the snow in strange patterns. The red crystal eyes of the monkey fan glinted knowingly from the middle of the pile.

Suddenly a triumphant cry rang out and everyone looked up to see Sebastian and Mesmer emerge from the blizzard. Behind them was a very creaky-looking cart being pulled by an extremely weather-beaten horse. The stocky creature had a matted brown mane and long tail, which dragged in the snow as it shambled along.

"We have transport for your works of genius!" Sebastian exclaimed. "A noble steed pulling a golden chariot!"

"Is that the best you could do?" Elizabeth said, making no attempt to disguise the contempt in her voice. "That has to be the oldest horse in Pinrut."

"Meet Turnip—so called because he'll do anything as long as you keep shoveling them in!"

Sebastian held up a sack by way of demonstration, plucked a withered turnip from inside and shoved it into the horse's mouth, who started to chew contentedly. Mesmer scuttled away in indignant horror as a few lumps fell from the horse's mouth, narrowly missing the dog's head.

Once the machines were packed onto the cart, Rufus and Madeline watched their parents say their good-byes.

None of them had ever been apart before. Their father was almost jaunty, but their mother was white-faced and clung to him for a long time.

When it was Mrs. Breeze's turn to hug Madeline good-bye, Philip took Rufus aside.

"Be watchful of Tullock, Ru," said his father, ruffling his neat hair. "Stay in the house. Use it to your advantage. When we leave, go inside and lock it down as the plans I gave you instruct. You'll both be safe."

"We *will* be all right, Mother," Madeline insisted behind them.

Elizabeth nodded and wiped her eyes, hunching her shoulders against the cold as Rufus stepped closer to her protectively.

"All right, Sunshine, let's get going." Philip pulled his cloak around him.

"You got all your tools?" Rufus asked, pointing at Madeline's toolbelt.

"Yes, and I'm going to practice while I'm away," Madeline said. "By the time I get back, I'll be better than you!"

Rufus laughed. "In your dreams, frost-face!"

Madeline grinned bravely and marched off to grab Turnip's harness before she started crying too. She hid her face in her scarf.

"People, we are about to unleash the floodgates of fortune!" Sebastian hollered with a sudden burst of enthusiasm. He held up his map and prodded it for show.

Elizabeth eyed the growing damp patches already spreading up her husband's boots—they looked suspiciously like one of Sebastian's pairs! She took a step toward the salesman.

"Mr. Silver, when this is done, I don't want you to come back here," she hissed. "Let my husband and daughter return without you."

Sebastian's bravado fell away. "Don't you trust me, Mrs. Breeze?" Sebastian asked.

"No, we don't," Rufus interjected firmly.

"The fanmakers will return to Pinrut safe and rich, I assure you," Sebastian said. Rufus and Elizabeth did not see the fingers crossed hopefully behind his back.

There was nothing more to say. Sebastian wedged the map into his hatband and joined Madeline and her father by the cart. Mesmer had already bounded out front, leading the way.

Madeline waved frantically at Rufus as the cart pulled off. Her mother blew them a kiss . . . and then the snowstorm came between them, and they could see one another no more.

"Come on, Mother, let's go inside," Rufus said.

# THIRTEEN

# Crossing the Fields

The blizzard parted to reveal a gray leviathan of a building. Thick columns supported a massive roof made up of crests and carved stonework. A motto in stone relief protruded over the immense iron doors—

**THE SUN SHINES WARM FOR US ALL**

It had obviously once been very grand, but now the columns were crumbling and icicles hung from every surface.

The westbound travelers trudged past. Sebastian let out a low whistle.

"Do you good to get away," he said. "I mean, look at the state of this dismal place."

"That was the Parliament building," Philip answered bitterly. "Fine people used to rule over Pinrut from there. Until they were driven out of power by Tullock and this blasted snow."

A dark helmeted figure passed one of the top-floor windows. Mesmer let out a low growl. Sebastian shuddered. "What was that?"

"It's a tin-head," Madeline said, her voice matter-of-fact. "One of Tullock's Hammer Squad—they live in there now."

Sebastian's eyes flicked back to the darkened building.

"Let's move along, shall we?" he said briskly. Market stalls lined the street farther along. They were stocked with worn, random goods, and the stallholders looked tired and drawn, bundled up in ragged woolen clothing against the bitter cold. Philip tried to keep his head down as they passed by.

"She kicked you out then, Breeze?" bellowed a gruff woman in her fifties. "About time."

"Thank you for your concern, Mrs. Stoop, but I'm merely taking a fan-related business trip," Philip replied with a strained smile.

"I think it might be best if you forgot the fanmaking side of things, Mr. Breeze. If you don't mind me saying," another stallholder offered.

"We do mind you saying," Madeline countered, her eyes blazing white hot.

"You Breezes are lunatics!" a filthy man behind a stall full of rusty buckets yelled.

Madeline reached out a comforting hand to her father's hunched back. The market street seemed so much longer than she remembered. "Can't this horse go any faster?" she snapped.

"Seems like your father's a big hit around here," Sebastian remarked.

"They're jealous because he's still standing up to Tullock," Madeline said, her eyes flicking from one sullen stallholder to the next. "They've all given in to that horrible snow-dome and turned against each other in competition to survive—so they're full of hatred and despair. I feel sorry for them."

An elderly man with a squinty expression jabbed his finger at her father from behind his stall of gnarled old sticks.

"You're wasting your time, Breeze. You can still kneel. You should be in the fields. What gives you the right to be any different from the rest of us?"

"Where *are* these fields, anyway?" Sebastian asked. "Can they be that bad?"

Madeline let out a long, expressive sigh. "You'll see."

The tall wrought-iron gates of Pinrut loomed over the little group as they finally left town. Beyond the gates stretched mile upon mile of flat, snow-covered fields. Madeleine pointed. Everywhere, as far as the eye could see, people knelt and scrabbled in the frozen dirt. The sense of despair and fatigue was as thick as the snowflakes that fell with unfailing constancy on the diggers.

Sebastian could not believe what he was seeing.

"All these people . . . ," he said.

"Welcome to the turnip and parsnip fields of Pinrut," Madeline said.

"And Tullock owns *all* this?" Sebastian asked.

Madeline's father nodded into the middle distance. There, astride a massive black stallion, draped in a bloodred woolen cloak, was Tullock.

"My father refused to work here," Philip said. "And while there's a ray of hope, I shall live by the same code."

"Come on, let's go before the snow-dome sees us!" Madeline urged, pulling on Turnip's harness in a bid to get the horse moving faster.

But as they all pushed on, a stray gust of wind suddenly snatched at the map that was wedged into Sebastian's hatband. He did not notice as it was whisked away across the fields.

It flicked and twisted in the breeze and flew within inches of Tullock's ear. He reached out and grabbed at the fluttering paper, then peered down at it in confusion.

But realization soon dawned. It was a map, and the desert town of Tresedira was circled. For a moment Tullock seemed worried, but as he looked up, he saw three faint figures on the horizon, struggling with a horse and cart. A dog bounded around the group. Tullock plucked a polished telescope from his pocket and raised it to his eye. Philip's face loomed large. So the fanmaker was leaving. Tullock allowed himself a small but very satisfied smile.

FOURTEEN

# A Rusted Centripetal Rose-Hub

In the Breeze house, Rufus was flicking through sheets of complicated drawings and instructions. His father had not wanted to be parted from Grandfather's notebook, so he had copied out the house defense mechanisms for Rufus before he left. Rufus sensed his mother anxiously trying to follow the twisting diagrams over his shoulder. The wind howled outside, making the fire in the grate flicker.

"Well, Rufus, at least we have firewood," Elizabeth said.

Rufus followed his mother's gaze to the pile of wood that had once been the grandfather-clock case. "Will Tullock come here once he knows Father's gone?" he couldn't help asking.

His mother looked at him. "Why would he? The next payment's not due for a while."

But Rufus knew it was a lie. He was sure Tullock would take this opportunity to try to tear the Breeze house asunder. Well, Rufus would not let that happen. All they had to do was lock down the house and sit tight. They had enough turnips to last them weeks. They would survive even if their taste buds didn't.

With one last, longing look at his workbench and the plans for a new fan he and Madeline had been developing, Rufus turned to his father's spiraling pencil lines in earnest. He ran his finger across the paper as though choosing a route on a map. "There seems to be a lever somewhere in the basement. Pull it, and iron shutters fan out over all the windows and front door and metal grilles unfold in the chimneys. Nobody will be able to get in!"

Elizabeth gave a grateful smile. "Let's go find that lever."

His father's basement workshop had grown over the years into a dense labyrinth of tools, machines and materials. It took Rufus a good hour to rummage his way through the creative debris and reach the wooden panel embedded in the back wall. With the flip of a chisel, the panel clattered to the floor. Peering into the recess beyond, Rufus could just make out a metal lever pitted with rust and covered in cobwebs.

"It looks like it hasn't been used in a while," Rufus called back to his mother.

"It's *never* been used," she said. "These defenses were always meant for only the most unusual or . . . desperate of circumstances."

His mother's unsettled tone made Rufus feel for a moment as though he were drifting slightly, hovering above the ground, the comfort of gravity banished. The four of them had always been so close, and now his father and sister were going far away. Still, he was determined to be strong—he was the man of the house now, and he'd do his best to live up to it.

He gripped the handle with two hands and tugged with all his might. A rasping noise like dry leaves being rubbed together was swiftly replaced with a sharp twang . . . as though something somewhere had snapped.

His mother swept over to the stairs and stormed up them. Her voice rang down from above.

"The windows aren't covered—the door's still just a door!"

Rufus gritted his teeth and clenched his fingers.

"Bring the plans!" he called up.

Twenty minutes later there was a jagged hole in all the walls halfway around his father's workshop. Rufus had hacked his way through them with an ice pick in an effort to find the link in the chain that had failed—the reason the defense mechanism had not been sprung. Finally, he stepped back with a weary sigh. He pointed at an intricate circular component made up of several dozen heart-shaped metal pieces. The surface was brown with orange flecks and had the texture of pressed wet sugar.

"It's as I thought," he said, his heart sinking. "The

centripetal rose-hub has rusted. The steam from Father's piston saw probably got in there."

His mother held a candle close and peered at the corroded part. "Can you fix it?"

Rufus coughed and the whole piece disintegrated into a reddish dust that cascaded to the floor and drifted up against his mother's shoes.

"Nope. We're gonna have to go out and find a new one," Rufus said.

Madeline, her father and Sebastian continued their passage through the vegetable fields in reverential silence. The diggers did not look up as they passed, lost as they were in the effort and pain of breaking through the frozen earth with their ragged fingers. Even Mesmer seemed to feel the gloom stretching over everything like an invisible mist, and he led the way with his furry head bowed, ears pressed back against his head.

The flat fields appeared to stretch for miles, so it was a surprise when something vertical came into view, a huge telescopic pole that extended upward far into the snow clouds.

"Gracious, what's that?" Sebastian asked.

Just at that moment, with a deafening grinding noise, the pole started to compress downward into the ground. The top of it came into view, emerging from the clouds. At the top was a wooden platform, and sitting squarely on this platform was a tall greenhouse with tiny pointed turrets made of dull gray lead. Briefly, slabs of dazzling light seemed to be trapped inside it, flashing and reflecting off the panes of glass.

"Beautiful," Madeline breathed.

"That's the sunflower vault," her father explained. "For a few hours every day it's elevated above the snow clouds so that the sunflowers within can bathe in sunshine and grow."

Madeline watched the vault finally settle at ground level with a steam-powered hiss. The snowflakes that fell on its glass melted instantly in the warmth of the sun still trapped inside.

Twenty Hammer Squad members were stationed closely around the building.

"The florists of Pinrut obviously look after their wares," Sebastian commented drily.

"Nobody ever sees the flowers," Madeline piped up. "They're all made into sunflower tonic."

"Pinrutian flu developed when the unending snow came," her father added sadly. "It's deadly. The Tullocks hired someone to find a cure. They hit upon the sunflower. The energy sunflowers absorb from the sun is a powerful antidote to an illness born of freezing cold."

Madeline frowned. "But the Tullocks keep it all to themselves, even though they're not poor, cold and half starved like the rest of us, so *they* are never ill."

"You know, I'm really starting to think these Tullocks aren't such nice people," Sebastian said.

"We should give the tin-heads a wide berth in case they spot us." Madeline grabbed Turnip's harness and pulled him away toward the woods.

The trees closed in densely around them, their sparse limbs bowed by the weight of the ever-falling snow. Sebastian tugged his hat down tighter against the cold. As he did so he brushed his fingers over the band to check on the map. He couldn't feel it. Glancing furtively at Madeline and her father, he removed his hat and spun it around wildly. The map was gone.

"Everything all right, Mr. Silver?" Madeline asked as she observed the thin layer of snow building rapidly on his curly hair.

He gulped. "Er . . ." No—he wouldn't mention it. After all, they just had to keep traveling west, and he was pretty sure he had a compass somewhere in his satchel. He couldn't have his latest—and, he couldn't help thinking, most promising in a while—possibility of wealth turn back! Sebastian clapped his hat back on and grinned. "Everything's just dandy!" he proclaimed. "Our fortune awaits. Lead on, Mesmer, my faithful friend!"

FIFTEEN

# The Sinister Domain of Scratskin

Tullock was slumped in his favorite armchair, staring into the flames that flickered and leaped in the colossal fireplace. His mother sat opposite, stroking a badly stuffed cat in her lap, apparently unconcerned by its crossed eyes and bared yellow teeth.

"Don't get me wrong," Tullock finally said. His comment was the result of a rambling train of thought that had been making figure eights in his mind for the last half hour.

"Yeees," Aspid drawled.

"I'm glad Windy's leaving—but he had a cart with him."

"Hmm," Aspid replied.

"And the desert circled on a map."

"I know," his mother said.

Tullock sat up. "What? How do you know? I've only just told you."

"Monetary rewards and sweet intimidation—we Tullocks have built up quite a network of informers over the years."

"Well, you could have filled me in sooner," Tullock sulked. For a moment he sat in silent contemplation. Then he leaped up suddenly. The facts had fallen into place in his mind like pieces of toast being slotted into a toast rack.

"Argh! He's taken his fans with him," he snapped. "He's going to sell them!"

"Duh—yeees," Aspid rasped. She held out a paper bag to her son. "Chocolate-covered turnip?"

But Tullock was too busy pacing to even turn his nose up at the delicacy.

"Well, we can't have Windy coming back here with a fortune. That much I know," he muttered. "I'll have to send a few messages."

"Scratskin will do it."

Tullock shuddered. "No, I'm not talking to him. I'm fed up with all these stuffed animals." Tullock gestured around at the menagerie of frozen creatures bolted to the walls and lying across every available surface. "It's like living in some kind of zombified zoological garden."

"I quite like them," Aspid said, tickling the motionless cat on her lap under the chin. "You know, you shouldn't be scared of him, Tully."

Tullock leaped back as though stung. "Scared? Me?" He raised his jaw and thrust out his chest. "Let's put the lazy rascal to work, shall we?" He bounded over to a panel by the fireplace and pushed on it. A hidden door sprang open to reveal a tight, twisting staircase that led upward into blackness.

"Come along, Mother!" Tullock snapped.

"Very well," Aspid replied. "I'll come up with you . . . if you're still afraid."

"I am *not* afraid." Tullock glowered. "I, er, just want you to be there when I'm bawling out the wayward wretch."

"Ooh, wait for me!"

It was a long climb to the top of Scratskin's tower, and the whole way Aspid's knees clicked and Tullock's heart hammered in his throat. He didn't know why the servant unsettled him so, but he did. Finally they reached a cobwebby door. Primly, Tullock wrapped his handkerchief around his knuckles and gave a sharp rap. A voice that sounded like it belonged in a graveyard rattled back.

"Enter if you must."

Yes, Tullock thought as he went in, the voice was a large part of Scratskin's unsettling nature.

Aspid scuttled in behind her son, looking around with an almost glowing approval. Scratskin's room was like the inside of a giant snail shell. The walls were curved and wet, and etched with hundreds of scratches, as though something trapped had been trying to escape. The two windows were narrow horizontal slits, like the half-awake vigil of some wily old serpent. And there were more stuffed animals on rickety shelves.

Scratskin sat at a large desk in the greenish light of an oil lamp. His lips were drawn back in concentration in such a way that he looked even more skeletal than usual.

"Kindly stop what you are doing, Scratskin," Tullock said, trying to sound in charge. "Though . . . what *are* you doing?" He peered at the map of Reffinock forest that Scratskin was so intent on.

With a scowl, Scratskin folded it up and turned his bulging eyes toward his master.

"I'm considering locations for my latest special traps. I *will* catch the elusive Great Snow Bear one day, though I have failed so far. It will be a unique addition to my collection."

Aspid peered through one of the narrow window slits. In one direction she could see icebergs in the sea far, far below; in the other, the forest. "That's quite a view," she said. "I'd forgotten how high up you are, Scratskin."

"It affords me a bird's-eye view of the bear's usual domain."

But Tullock hadn't come to talk about bears.

"Scratskin, we've a few messages to send out west and—"

"Awaken, Ravenna!" Scratskin shrieked suddenly.

Tullock nearly fell backward in shock. His ears were still ringing as Scratskin whipped away a cloth to reveal a giant wrought-iron cage. Inside was an enormous black raven with beady eyes that held points of light so bright they seemed to burn through everything it glanced at.

"And the nature of this message?" Scratskin croaked. Tullock scribbled hurriedly on a few scraps of paper and gave them to Scratskin, who tied them to one of the raven's thick, leathery talons. He pulled the bird from the cage and let it settle on his bony forearm. Aspid surveyed the narrow windows again doubtfully, but Scratskin simply lurched over to a wall and with a sudden savage movement slammed his free fist through it. Stone bricks tumbled away into the churning ocean below and a flurry of snow blew into the room.

"That's coming out of his wages," Tullock mumbled to his mother, though quietly enough that Scratskin wouldn't hear.

"Scythe a trail across the sky like the shadow of death, my feathered messenger," Scratskin cried.

He flung the raven through the hole and it streaked away with a high-pitched caw.

Scratskin turned to Tullock and Aspid, his gangly form silhouetted against the snow falling behind him.

"Friend or not, Ravenna knows that if he fails me, I will be forced to add him to my collection . . ."

"Er, we'll be going now," Tullock mumbled, shuffling back toward the door.

"Thanks for your help," Aspid said, retreating also. "Love what you've done with the room."

# SIXTEEN

# Rufus on a Mission

Rufus stood by the front door dressed in a long brown cloak. His mother pulled the hood up to cover his face. She was shaking.

"Are you *sure* we can't fix it with things inside the house?" she asked.

"A centripetal rose-hub is really complicated, Mother," Rufus replied. "It's a unique universal joint that can control at least two dozen independent mechanical functions. It takes ten men with ten magnifying lenses and ten stopwatches ten days to choreograph the making of *one*. It's phenomenal."

"I see," Elizabeth said, though she didn't at all. "Can't we just bypass this hub thing?" she tried instead. "Pull the shutters down manually with a stick or something?"

Rufus shook his head. "Grandfather constructed the defenses so they couldn't be tampered with."

"Oh, I don't want you out there alone. I'm coming

with you," his mother said finally, turning to find her coat.

"Someone needs to stay in the house. If Tullock thinks it's been abandoned, he might take the hammer to it anyway. At least if you're here you can sweet-talk him," Rufus countered. Though he didn't want to go alone, he knew he had to. "I'll be quick," he added, trying to sound as brave as Madeline had when she'd set off earlier.

"Where will you go?"

"To the scrap quarter," Rufus replied. "Only place I can think of where they might have something so unusual." Elizabeth wrapped her arms around Rufus and squeezed.

"I'll be back soon," he said, twisting his sun-shaped cuff links for luck. "Lock this door after me."

"Be so, so careful," Elizabeth called as Rufus scurried away into the blizzard.

She slid the bolt back into place, feeling hollow inside. Her entire family was out in the elements, unprotected. She closed her eyes and wished for their safe and speedy return. But she had a nagging feeling that wishes were not going to be enough.

Rufus ran past the sinister Parliament building and on toward the main market street. It was a long way to the scrap quarter, and he wanted to get there and back as fast as he could.

The diggers were returning from the fields, and his own direction made him conspicuous—like a fish swimming upstream. They shuffled along the street, silent and drained. Snowflakes settled on their hunched shoulders. It was difficult for Rufus to make headway against the shambling tide too—the workers were exhausted but determined to get home to whatever little nourishment and warmth awaited them and the blissful respite of bed. In front of a particularly shabby-looking stall, Rufus ran straight into one of them. His hood fell back and he looked up into the grimy but noble face of an old neighbor, Henry Bugle, Arabella's husband, who stared back at him from under a worn-looking cap.

"Hello. What's a young Breeze doing out here?" Henry said.

"Nothing. Just running an errand." Rufus lowered his voice. "I have to get to the scrap quarter."

Henry's features suddenly became serious. "That's no place for a boy. In fact, you shouldn't be out of the house on your own at all, Rufus," he said, looking this way and that. "I'll take you home."

"No, it's all right, really," Rufus insisted.

"The Breeze family is certainly enjoying the fresh air today," called Mr. Pebble suddenly from behind his stall of gnarled sticks. "Mister and daughter left town earlier. Good riddance, I say."

"Be quiet, Pebble. And mind your own business—such

as it is," Henry barked. He shuffled around so that he stood between Rufus and Mr. Pebble, but the old stallholder edged nearer nonetheless.

"What's going on, boy?" Henry asked. His voice was gruff, but there was kindness and concern in it too.

Rufus found he was suddenly desperate to share his troubles. "Father and Madeline did leave today. They're heading west to try to sell fans where it's still hot," Rufus said. "It's a good thing. Really."

"But what are you doing out?" Henry asked.

"I need a centripetal rose-hub."

Henry raised his eyebrows. "Clement's defense mechanisms," he muttered under his breath. He leaned close to Rufus and lowered his voice still further. "All right, go to the scrap quarter. Talk to my cousin, Hayden Shacklefield. He should be able to help you."

"But how do you know about Grandfather's plans?" Rufus asked.

"It doesn't matter. Go and see my cousin now. Hurry!" Henry gave the boy a gentle but insistent shove. "Hug the shadows, Rufus. Talk to nobody else."

Rufus gave a curt nod, raised his hood once more and ran off, dodging his way through the crowd. Henry watched him go, his face grim.

And Mr. Pebble raised his eyebrows and settled back with a smug smile. He was old, but his hearing was exceptional. It always had been.

SEVENTEEN

# A Nightmarish Mountain

Tullock was sitting in his weather room at the base of the barometer tower. He liked to pass the time here just watching the snow fall in the glowing glass domes that acted as his window on Pinrut. But this evening he had eyes only for the Breeze house. He twisted a dial and the house grew bigger inside the dome as he zoomed in on it. With Philip gone, now was his chance, but how could he make Elizabeth see that life would be so much better with him, in his mansion?

"Send in the Hammer Squad. Demolish the house now."

Tullock spun around to see his mother standing in the doorway. She cracked her knuckles.

"Elizabeth is still in there," Tullock said.

"So? Mind you—your father used to send poisoned cake if he wanted to get rid of someone. Many a night I'd hear him in that kitchen with an egg whisk . . . genius." Aspid had a faraway look in her eyes.

"I don't want her dead!" Tullock exclaimed, leaping to his feet. "I want to win her over. I want her to inject a little life into this place! Anyway, Elizabeth wouldn't be stupid enough to eat cake that came through the mailbox."

Aspid wandered over to the glass dome behind Tullock and spun the dial with a vicious twist of her wrist. The view of the Breeze house suddenly receded into nothing more than a speck. "I think this little 'crush' is starting to cloud your judgment, Tully," she said.

"It's *not* a crush!" Tullock snapped. "Elizabeth's the most beautiful woman in Pinrut. So naturally she should be with the most handsome and accomplished man. No one else. She can't be truly happy when she deserves so much more."

"So you're not sending cake?"

"No! There has to be a better way," Tullock mused.

"Meat loaf?" Aspid suggested.

"If only I could lure her up here somehow," Tullock went on. "*Show* her how things could be." He spun the dial again so that the house's image filled the dome once more.

"Now you're warming up," Aspid said, her eyes shining. "In fact, word has it the Breeze boy is running loose in Pinrut, headed toward the scrap quarter, apparently." And she made no attempt to hide the glee in her voice.

As the cool light of evening dimmed, Madeline and her father hefted and heaved on Turnip's harness, the blizzard still dancing its frenzied waltz around them. They had passed through the woods without too much difficulty, but now the snow-laden slopes of Mount Rumble were making progress more difficult. It was an unforgiving place—full of sharp rocks, dense snowdrifts and deep howling ravines to threaten the unprepared traveler.

The cart's wheels were getting stuck in the thick snow and Turnip was finding it difficult to keep it moving. At the point they had reached, the mountain fell away on both sides of the cart in two sheer, plunging drops. Under the rocking cart's canvas covering, the fans jostled and rattled, whistled and clicked, almost as if they were talking to each other.

"Mr. Silver, could you give us a hand here!" Madeline called out through the snowy silence, stamping her crampons down hard for added traction.

Sebastian was up ahead muttering to Mesmer and intermittently checking a compass, which was now dangling on a chain around his neck.

"Hmm, very interesting," Sebastian mumbled under his breath. "You know, Mesmer, I'm a great believer in Father Fate, Lady Luck and Professor Providence. Too much stuffy planning or nitpicky organization stifles adventure. Know what I mean?"

Mesmer looked up at Sebastian, his furry blue brow furrowed. His tail drooped. Trouble was brewing and he knew it.

"Mr. Silver! We need you to help!" Madeline shouted again. How infuriating the man was, she thought as she had a quick anxious nibble of her little fingernail. Sebastian strode back toward the horse and cart.

"Is this really the best way to go?" she asked as he joined them.

"Yes—now that you mention it, Sunshine, dragging a cart up a mountain does seem a bit foolish if you can go around," her father added.

Sebastian busied himself with scrabbling snow away from the front wheels of the cart.

"Mr. Silver?" Madeline prompted. Sebastian stood up straight and squinted at the age-old peaks and ridges, affecting a weary wisdom.

"You can't go around a mountain like this," he said in hushed tones. "It'll mock you if you try. It craves a worthy opponent. Which is why it *demands* we go right over the top. It'll respect us all the more for it."

"Sorry we asked," Madeline said drily. But her brother's warning words about Mr. Silver—and looking after her father—were still fresh in her ears. She had to be the sensible one, like Rufus would be—and this just didn't seem like a very sensible route.

Sebastian only smiled beneficently, her sarcasm lost on him.

"Don't be sorry, Madeline. It's perfectly natural to be

curious." Desperate, Madeline gave her father a forceful look.

"Er, can I look at the map, Sebastian?" he asked in response.

"Sorry, Mr. Breeze. I'm captain of the coordinates," Sebastian said firmly. "Can't have too many cooks peering at them, can we?"

Madeline moved closer to Sebastian and the compass hanging around his neck.

"No, really, can I see the map?" her father went on.

"No," Sebastian replied. "It's my map. And you are being childish with your fervent desire to look for a golden route with no potholes that DOESN'T EXIST on MY MAP!"

"I don't expect to see a route, golden or otherwise," Philip replied indignantly. "Just a better way than this perilous mountain pass, as my daughter suggested. Now give me the map, please."

"I don't have it," Sebastian mumbled. He looked down at his boots. He noticed with regret that the cold and wet had discolored them—it was so difficult to look one's best in these conditions—

"What?" Madeline exclaimed.

"I've lost it! All right?" Sebastian blurted. "It's been whisked away by the map fairies!"

"So how in the name of Endless Winter do you know where we're going?" Madeline's father demanded.

"Wake up, sleepy man! I have a compass!" Sebastian said. "All we have to do is head west."

"But there's no needle in the compass!" Madeline pointed out. She looked at Sebastian and gave a small disappointed shake of her head. At her heels, Mesmer joined in.

Rapidly, Sebastian covered the compass with his hand. "There *is* a very *high-quality* needle in this compass," he retorted. "But it does, for now, seem to have become detached. A few of my customers had the same problem. Never buy navigational aids from a man who's wearing his trousers around the wrong way is my advice."

Madeline watched her father's face fall. "I've endangered my entire life's work on this nightmarish mountain," he lamented. "And now we have to turn back . . . Tresedira is already lost to us, as are all those lovely sweltering people . . ."

Dejectedly, he kicked a rock, which flew into the air, then plummeted down a dark, plunging ravine like a grape falling into the mouth of a whale. "Ow! I thought these boots were meant to be impenetrable!" he added.

"Look, we're heading west, I know it," Sebastian said quickly. "There's really no need to panic. See the two tall pointy rocks up near the peak? I am utterly convinced that once we pass between those, our journey will be a mischievous delight, a stolen moment with a cream cake, a slide into a featherbed," he gabbled desperately. The fur above Mesmer's eyes flattened into a frown. The more flowery Sebastian's words became, the bigger the mess, usually.

But Madeline looked up at the two sentries of rock, blurred by the blizzard yet solid in the distance. Maybe they were the gateway to the perfect path to this Tresedira place. What else could they try now anyway?

"Come on, Father. We have to keep moving. And," she said, gritting her teeth, "I'm sure Mr. Silver is right about the rocks." She forced a smile. "Imagine the faces in Tresedira, Father, when they see your fans."

Philip brightened immediately.

"Give the horse another turnip," Sebastian suggested sheepishly. "He's like a powerhouse when he's popping those little beauties."

EIGHTEEN

# Under Attack!

The scrap quarter was full of strange buildings made of rusty sheets of metal that seemed to be held together by old, bent cutlery. Windows were barrel hoops, and chimneys were nothing more than buckets with the bottoms sawn off. Piles of machine parts lay buried in the snow behind every dwelling. This place had once been a honeypot of fine mechanical merchandise drawing craftspeople from far and wide. It was one of the reasons Breezes had been living in Pinrut for generations. But since the snow had arrived, people just came to dump and swap old parts, and to get household goods patched up cheaply.

However, Rufus knew there were still gems to be found among the junk. Sometimes even components from dumped Breeze fans that had been bought by the villagers in better times. Rufus had been here before with his father, and the place had seemed exciting and mysterious, but now as he scurried along alone, searching for

Hayden Shacklefield's workshop, it seemed dark and forbidding.

Finally, Rufus found it—a squat copper dome held together by hundreds of rivets. A sign hanging over it read

**SHACKLEFIELD'S EMPORIUM OF MAGNIFICENT MECHANICALS**

With a sense of relief, Rufus stepped up to the door and pulled on what looked like a lavatory chain. Tinny chimes resounded inside. A muffled voice drifted back.

"Enter if you must."

Rufus took a deep breath and pushed open the door. He hoped Mr. Shacklefield was going to be helpful. The lighting was so dim inside that Rufus had to be careful he didn't trip over the nails, cogs and springs and pieces of machinery that were scattered everywhere. At the far end of the room was a wonky desk, and sitting at it was a man wearing a large black hat with a wide brim that completely obscured his features. Rufus made his way over with tentative steps. A few lit candles caused hundreds of reflected darts of light to bounce off shiny metallic surfaces until it seemed to Rufus as if he were walking among the stars. He felt odd, giddy and dislocated. The man did not raise his head, so Rufus had no choice but to talk to the top of his hat.

"Are you Hayden Shacklefield?"

"Yes, I am," came the reply. The voice was deep yet hollow, like a ball bearing running around the bottom of a bucket.

"Then I believe you can help me," Rufus said. "Henry Bugle sent me. I need a centripetal rose-hub. Do you have one?"

"Why?"

Rufus felt a growing sense of unease. "Do I have to tell you why I need one to buy one?" he asked.

"It will tell me what type you need," the man countered.

Rufus started to edge away from the desk, putting one careful foot behind the other. Something was wrong. There was only *one* type of centripetal rose-hub; they were *unique*. And any real scrap merchant would know that.

"Why don't you answer me, boy?" The man was rising now, moving out from behind the desk.

"Well, er, a centripetal rose-hub is a centripetal rose-hub . . . There *are* no types."

"Are you suggesting you know more than I do about mechanical matters?" the man asked. He was closing in on Rufus.

"It would appear so," Rufus replied, retreating faster, his steps gathering pace to match the accelerating rhythm of his heart. Something was *very* wrong.

The next sequence of events happened in an instant.

Rufus saw a reflection in a sheet of polished steel: another man, bound and gagged and crammed into a corner—Hayden Shacklefield. He saw the brim of the mysterious man's hat rise to reveal a sight that sent tremors down his spine, a pale, gaunt face with bulbous, unblinking eyes . . . and then Scratskin lunged, his long clawlike fingers speeding toward Rufus like daggers. Rufus stumbled back and reached for his toolbelt. With a skillful quick-draw and parry, he blocked Scratskin's talons with a mallet. Tullock's manservant let rip a guttural cry as one of his nails sank deep into its wood. But even as he did so, he lashed out sideways and the tool went flying from Rufus's hands.

Rufus turned and ran for the door. He threw it open and dashed out into the snow. But Scratskin was right there with him, his rancid breath now white and misty on the back of Rufus's neck.

The freezing air burned in Rufus's lungs as he pounded through the scrap quarter and back into town.

"Help me!" he cried, but the broken people of Pinrut slunk back behind the safety of their closed doors. Scratskin was fast. Rufus could feel the tips of his terrible fingers occasionally grazing his cloak. He tried to think as he ran. Where should he go? It could be a mistake to lead Tullock's servant back to his home, under the circumstances, but maybe there he would have a better chance of fighting this apparition off.

"I always catch my prey," Scratskin rasped from behind him. His voice had an edge like a newly sharpened blade.

"You can't catch a Breeze, chiller man!" Rufus panted back with a bravado he didn't feel.

The long fingers reached out again for Rufus's cloak and almost caught it.

Rufus put on a burst of speed. He was belting past the now empty market stalls. Thinking fast, he pulled a disused barrel over and turned briefly to watch already icy water spill across the street, freezing instantly.

A second later Scratskin went flying over the ice and clattered into a stall, a pile of tangled limbs.

Rufus allowed himself a satisfied smile and sped on. Madeline would have appreciated that move . . . But victory was short-lived as Scratskin quickly snarled back to life and came after him again.

By the time the old Parliament building came into view, Rufus could feel his legs beginning to tire, the snow weighing them down. If he could just keep up the pace—behind him, Scratskin was finally slowing—he might make it.

But Scratskin had very definite other ideas as he pulled a dart-pipe from the inside pocket of his long gray coat.

Rufus's heart gave a hopeful leap as the familiar silhouette of home started to take shape through the veil of ever-falling snow. He was almost there. He could see the door now—and the sun motif on it seemed to radiate a real warmth.

But then he felt a sharp sting in his calf. He turned to see a small dart buried in his flesh. A numb feeling began to spread up to his knee. He fell forward. He could no longer feel his leg. What was happening to him? Scratskin, his parchment lips stretched back into a victorious gloat, swaggered over, waving his dart-pipe mockingly.

Then he plucked a small horn from his pocket and blew into it. Within moments four black stallions thundered into view, drawing their beetle-like carriage. Rufus felt helplessly numb as Scratskin bundled him inside and leaped into the driver's seat. He didn't see Scratskin pick up a crossbow from the seat next to him, aim it at the door of the Breeze house and fire a bolt into the heart of the wooden sun design. He didn't see the message that unfurled from it. If he had, he would have felt even worse.

A savage crack of the whip urged the stallions onward, and soon the carriage was nothing more than a gray smudge receding into the distance.

A heartbeat later, Elizabeth drew back the bolt on the door and took a cautious step outside.

"Rufus!" she called. "Is that you?" The message fluttered in the corner of her vision. She spun around and ripped it away from the crossbow bolt with a shaky hand.

Dearest Elizabeth,

Your son is visiting me. You are most welcome to join us.

Kind regards,

Bartholomew Tullock

# NINETEEN

# The Great Glacier

Madeline doubled over, panting and catching her breath. The icy expanse of the Great Glacier stretched out before them. Wedged in a valley at least two miles across, the glacier's billions of tons of hard ice creaked and ground away at the rock walls on either side of it, even as they stood there.

It had taken a good few hours of heaving and coaxing to get Turnip and the cart up to the ridge where the two pointed rocks stood. And now, as Madeline looked out over the indigo crests and undulating valleys that dropped away darkly into the bowels of the glacier, she began to gnaw on her finger, horrified. This was the place Tullock sent people who'd displeased him—to die frozen and alone, presumably. Certainly no one ever came back from it. It was unnavigable and possibly, if Tullock was to be believed, unending. If Mr. Silver was to be believed, it wasn't. But that didn't give them much choice! Oh, why had they come this way? Madeline shot a disapproving look at Mr. Silver. Rufus had been so right about him.

But Sebastian only gestured wildly at the glacier. "We go on, no?"

For her father's sake, Madeline bit her tongue for the moment at Mr. Silver's ill-considered enthusiasm, though she continued to glower.

Her father was kinder. "How, er . . . how are we going to get a horse and cart across this, Sebastian?"

"There I might have to concede," Sebastian replied, stroking his chin as he mused on the problem. Mesmer was lying low on the snow, growling suspiciously in the direction of the glacier, but Sebastian ignored him. "Let's ditch the cart!"

"And what about all the fans?" Madeline asked, eyebrows raised.

"We'll wrap them up in sacking as best we can and drag them across!"

"Drag them across," Philip repeated faintly, horror-struck at the thought. "Precision machines bounced and scraped over solid ice. Now, why didn't I think of that?"

"Don't worry. We'll find the most level route," Sebastian offered. "Come on! That crummy old cart was holding us back anyway."

"I thought it was a 'golden chariot,'" Madeline snapped.

"What dingbat said that?" Sebastian replied, blinking with innocence.

There has to be a more practical way, thought Madeline, ignoring Mr. Silver. If Rufus were here, they'd think of something together, but now it was up to her.

Earlier, Madeline had set the butterfly fan going and attached it by a string to the cart. All this time it had bobbed merrily in the air above them, its colored glass wings batting the snow away and its quiet clicks soothing her. And, suddenly, as she looked at it, seeking inspiration, she knew.

"We could break up the cart and make a kind of sled," she offered.

"Of course," her father exclaimed.

"Even better, if we attach some of the stronger fans to the back of it, it should glide quite easily across the ice." Madeline grinned proudly.

"Your daughter is a genius!" Sebastian declared. "Let's chop the cart up immediately! Now, I've got a foldaway ax in my bag somewhere."

As dawn broke and the snow-filled sky shifted to a lighter shade of gray, Madeline headed out onto the ice, leading a shivering Turnip and a makeshift sled.

"I've heard about glaciers," Sebastian said, cutting some steps into a frozen incline with his ice pick. "Do not, whatever you do, fall into a crevasse. They drop about two hundred feet into a narrow point, and if you fall in, you'll probably break your pelvis, then die slowly, stuck. Of course, if you're lucky, you fall into one that leads all the way down to the river that runs through the belly of the glacier, but then you'd probably get hit by the rocks and debris in the churning water and drown anyway, or failing that, you'd freeze to death fairly rapidly."

"Thanks for the warning, Mr. Silver," Madeline said eventually. "And for scaring the living daylights out of us," she added under her breath, though her father seemed remarkably unfazed now that they were on their way once more.

Progress was a little slow as Sebastian searched out the more level parts of the glacier. It was made slower by him having to carry Mesmer, his furry face buried in his paws—the dog had been strangely reluctant to venture out onto the ice. Madeline had to admit, if only to herself, that she couldn't blame him.

Following Sebastian's route, Madeline persuaded Turnip across the slippery landscape. Her father had hastily crafted some horse crampons from nails and leather strapping he had in his toolbox so the horse did at least have some traction on the glassy surface. Two dozen of the more powerful fans flapped and whirred above and behind the sled, pulling it upward on strings and propelling it onward, making it lighter and easier to maneuver.

Madeline noticed her father checking on them anxiously at regular intervals as the snowflakes fluttered and danced in the air around them.

They were some way out on the glacier when a more sinister noise rose above the busy chatter of the fans: a pulsing, surging whine that spread across the ice. Sebastian stopped in his tracks. Mesmer whimpered in his arms.

"What in the name of all things weird and wiggy is that?"

"Look!" exclaimed Madeline, pointing off to one side as her stomach did a little flip of fear.

Shooting up from small holes all over the glacier were shimmering cones of icy, white vapor, frosty tornados over ten feet high. They spun at great speed, their innards a glittering, churning mass of arctic-blue ice particles and pieces of rock, before disappearing back below the glacier surface. There were dozens of them, and the noise they emitted made the hairs on Madeline's neck stand on end. Turnip was starting to buck and flinch, making the sled twitch alarmingly.

"What are they?" Philip wondered.

"Shoofas," Madeline replied, her eyes darting from one to another, concern growing.

"You know what they are?" her father asked in surprise.

"No. It's just the noise they're making," Madeline

replied as she gnawed on another nail. "Shoofa, shoofa, shoofa."

That was indeed the noise they were making as they burst forth again, some of them nearer the travelers this time.

"Something to do with the pressure under the ice?" Madeline speculated.

"Some sort of strange weather phenomenon?" Philip observed.

"No kidding, professors. But what happens if they keep heading this way?" Sebastian asked.

Madeline snapped a small piece of wood off the end of the sled and threw it as far as she could. A moment later a shoofa erupted underneath it, drew it up inside its frantic whirl, then spat it out. Madeline watched the now frozen baton fly halfway across the glacier and disappear into a crevasse. She gulped.

"They look really rather dangerous," Sebastian said as he headed back toward Madeline and her father. The hackles were rising on the back of Mesmer's neck and he barked his agreement. "Madeline, I suspect you haven't got long to figure out what we should do next."

"What?" Madeline exclaimed.

But a moment later Sebastian was proved horribly right. A shoofa ruptured the ice immediately beneath him, engulfing Mr. Silver and Mesmer instantly. Madeline gasped. Instinctively she stepped toward them, but her father grabbed her back, and they watched grimly as Sebastian and Mesmer became nothing more than a blue-and-yellow blur inside the screaming icy whirlwind. In the next instant Sebastian and a howling Mesmer were thrown high into the air—far across the glacier. They landed out of sight.

# TWENTY

# A Magnificent Beast

Elizabeth struggled toward the snow-laden forest, following Scratskin's already half-obscured carriage tracks. She knew that with their home empty it was very likely Tullock would destroy it, that this was a trap, but she at least had to try to rescue her son.

With a determination that defied the thick snow underfoot, Elizabeth ran along the track that led through the Reffinock forest to Tullock's cliff-top mansion. She felt focused, fueled by the injustice of it all. How dare this ogre of a man take her son!

The trees closed in around her, oily black arms with frosty white sleeves of snow pointed at her, mocking. Was she really going to take on the might of Bartholomew Tullock alone?

The emerald vulgarity of Tullock's abode was just now appearing in the inky spaces between the tangled branches. She would soon be there.

But suddenly an enormous, hulking creature shambled

out of the woods and stopped in front of Elizabeth. It was the Great Snow Bear.

Its thick white fur clung to mighty slabs of well-honed muscle. Its four legs were stout and solid like rock, and its head was huge and somehow regal. To its shoulder it was double Elizabeth's height.

Some would say it was a rare honor to see the creature—it was so private and perfectly camouflaged. No one knew where it came from, but glimpses had started a few years after the unending snowfall began. These were not, however, ideal circumstances for a privileged sighting. Face-to-face, alone and unprotected. Elizabeth froze as the mighty animal raised its moist, black snout and bellowed.

Chunks of snow fell from the limbs of trees overhead, thudding onto the track in dull surrender. The bear roared again, enraged. Elizabeth could feel the vibration of its bellow resonating through her body. She felt little more than a willowy reed before it. But her desperate desire to reach her son had not diminished. She held firm.

"Out of my way!" she cried. "I'm not in the mood!" The bear stopped midroar. What was this strange, small, noisy creature that did not run from him? Elizabeth's heart hammered in her chest as she locked her gaze with the bear's, but she stood her ground. "I said, out of my way."

The bear held her glance for a moment, intrigued,

almost . . . enchanted. Then, with a puzzled moan, it shambled off into the forest on the other side of the track. Elizabeth was trembling. She remembered to breathe, then shakily resumed her dash along the carriage tracks.

Rufus struggled against the viselike grip of the hideous Scratskin, his mind racing. The paralyzing poison from the dart had worn off, but Scratskin frog-marched Rufus into the main hall of the Tullock mansion with disconcerting ease nonetheless. Tullock was pacing up and down impatiently, lost in thought, but he stopped when he saw Rufus.

"Ah, the spawn of Breeze! How good of you to join us!" he gloated.

"It's not like I had much choice," Rufus replied, determined to stand up to Tullock as he had seen his father do—however much he quaked inside.

"Choice, my dear boy, is for the privileged few," Tullock declared. "Not the weak-minded majority."

"You tell him, Tully," Aspid hissed from her armchair by the fire, where she was painting her thick, crusty toenails with a brush attached to a long stick. The nail polish she was using looked like blood.

Rufus recoiled. Even Tullock recoiled.

"Can't you do that in your room, Mother?"

"It's my house," Aspid snapped back.

"You've missed a bit, my lady," Scratskin added.

Rufus twisted himself free of Scratskin's grip. "Why am I here?" he demanded.

"It's not your job to be curious, boy!" Tullock barked. "It's your job to do as I say, live as I say, *think* as I say!"

"You can't tell me what to think!" Rufus retorted. "My thoughts are my own!"

"Ah, how I pity you. To have these deluded ideas forced upon you by a clearly insane father," Tullock mocked. "A father who has now abandoned you." A wave of dread rose in Rufus's throat. Tullock knew that he and his mother were alone. He fought hard to maintain his composure.

"You don't understand my father because your mind is frozen," Rufus declared. "So what is it you want now?"

"What could I possibly want?" Tullock replied. "I already have everything."

"I don't believe you do. Are you going to destroy our house?"

Tullock gazed at Rufus with amusement. "Your father's not around to pay the debt so I can do as I wish."

"My mother's still there. She'll find a way to protect it. She won't leave it!" Rufus blurted. He swallowed his panic.

Tullock allowed himself a dry chuckle. "I think I know your mother better than you do, boy."

"The Breeze family will never bow to your will, Tullock!" Rufus exclaimed. "You're an abominable tyrant and we stand united against you."

Tullock raised his eyebrows. "Oh, if only you knew, Rufus," he taunted. "But I tire of this fruitless banter." Tullock feigned a yawn. "Scratskin, take him to a holding cell in my prison."

TWENTY-ONE

# A Grim Discovery in the Ice

Just as suddenly as they'd arrived, the shoofas were gone again and the only noise was that of the ordinary wind whipping across the ice and the whirr of the Breeze fans.

"I don't know how long we've got before the shoofas come back," Madeline said, "but we have to go and search for Mr. Silver and Mesmer." Her father gazed anxiously at the contents of the sled.

"Not sure I want to risk the fans by . . ." He faltered when he saw Madeline's expression. "Of course. But I should go and search for them alone, Sunshine," he said finally. "And if anything happens to me, you turn around and head home with the fans and—"

"I'm coming with you, Father!" Madeline was firm. "You may need me. It'll be quicker without the sled, but if they're still alive, they could be injured—you can't carry them both on your own."

"You know, for a moment you sounded just like your

mother," her father said with a small smile. "All right then, we'll go together."

Madeline breathed a sigh of relief. Quickly she plucked an attractive, old-fashioned fan made from gleaming feathers off the sled and tucked it into her pocket, thinking it might make a soothing talisman on their perilous rescue mission.

They left Turnip and the fans—reluctantly—on a flat portion of ice, with the only turnip they had, the rest being in the satchel over Sebastian's shoulder. Then Madeline and her father set out cautiously across the ice. By now they were so cold Madeline could hear her teeth chattering in time to their steps, and she couldn't help noticing her father's lips were worryingly blue. She wriggled her fingers inside her gloves to warm them and peered into the unending white toward the point where they thought they had seen Sebastian and Mesmer land. But with such an expanse of ice and platinum cloud it was hard to tell where the horizon ended and the sky began. Her father hacked steps into the rising and falling flanks of sloping ice with an ice pick, and Madeline carefully followed her father's trail. And although they were moving quickly, Madeline was very watchful for the dark blue gaping crevasses that riddled the glacier, and always listening for the shoofas' return. It was a long trek but they pushed on, pausing only once to watch a hideous-looking raven streak overhead, its black feathers stark against the milky sky. Something about it made Madeline shudder.

Surprisingly, it was Sebastian's useless compass that told them where to find him. Madeline spotted it sparkling at the mouth of an ice cave.

"They must have tumbled down here," she said, staring into its bruised indigo gloom.

The interior surfaces of the glacier cave were even colder, and so wet and translucent that they seemed to give off their own light. Madeline and her father crouched and slithered and skidded downward, neither speaking, neither admitting to the other that their mouths were dry and their hearts were pattering like balls bouncing down steps. There was no point, Madeline told herself. It wouldn't change the fact that they had to go on, to keep looking.

At last the cave opened up and leveled out. Madeline and her father both stood upright, and she gasped at the sheer scale of the cavern before them. It was a natural palace made of ice. From the ceiling just above them hundreds of enormous icicles dripped cold water into blue, mournful-looking pools below. Madeline noticed something small and dark suspended within one of the cave's smooth ice walls.

"What's that?" Madeline asked.

"Hmm? I don't know, Sunshine," her father replied distractedly.

Madeline moved closer.

"Oh no!" She reached out and touched the ice. Held deep within was a copper sun pendant. She had known the man who used to wear it. She felt sick. "All those who were banished here by Tullock must be all around us, lost to the glacier." A tear trickled down her face and froze at her chin. "What if Mr. Silver and Mesmer . . ." She couldn't finish the sentence.

"Let's just find them and go," her father urged nervously.

Madeline sniffed and nodded her head more firmly, then began to look around. It didn't take long to find the yawning crevasse even deeper inside the cave and the fresh scuff marks on one of its lips as if someone or something had recently fallen in. Sure enough, a little way down it, a man and his dog were wedged onto a narrow ice shelf, half embedded in the ice wall above it. Mesmer was stuck at an angle upside down, his tail pointing at the ceiling and his eyes wild at the indignity. Sebastian was frozen in a state of alarm; his expressive hands seemed suspended in a state of hasty, if failed, negotiation. But Mesmer's black button nose was still free from the ice, and Sebastian's whole head and neck were yet at liberty. There was a chance . . .

"They're still alive!" Madeline blurted out. "I'm sure of it!"

"H-h-h-hurry!" Sebastian seemed to breathe.

A sudden surging noise echoed through the cave. Madeline looked down with a shudder. She could see sparkling shapes shifting in the ice below. The shoofas were back. If she didn't act quickly, they would all perish in exactly the way that snow-dome, Tullock, would have wished. She thought of her brother. He wouldn't hang around. He wouldn't give Tullock the satisfaction. He'd organize!

"Lower me down, Father!" Madeline urged, pointing to the coiled rope on her father's toolbelt.

"This is madness," he worried. But he did as she said. Madeline lit her blowtorch as she descended into the crevasse, her father leaning backward and digging his crampons into the ice above. When she drew level with Sebastian, his icy lashes were open though his eyes were glazed.

"You c-came after us?" he chattered disbelievingly. "Why, after everything . . . ? No one ever . . ."

"Shush now, Mr. Silver," Madeline said briskly as she drew her blowtorch with the utmost care around Mesmer's outline. Rivulets of warm water flowed from the ice beneath its heat. "You're rambling." The ice around Sebastian started to melt a little too. With a gasp like a swimmer who breaks the water's surface after a long underwater swim, he began to wriggle against his freezing confinement. Above them, Madeline heard a shoofa whoosh its way through the cave, but her father and the rope stayed steady.

"The shoofa, it threw us . . . ," Mr. Silver muttered as he wriggled, "against the icy wall . . . winded . . . stuck to the ice . . . and then everything went cold and dark . . . Argh! Mesmer, our legend cannot end here . . ."

A shoofa suddenly erupted above, only feet from Madeline's father this time. "Mr. Silver, we have to go," Madeline said firmly. "Can you get out?" She turned off her blowtorch as the shivering dog fell free and into her arms, his blue hair sticking out in frost-coated tufts.

"We need to go *now*," Madeline urged.

Sebastian had managed to wrench his arms and a leg free. "But I'm so tired," he slurred. "Let's have a picnic right here. Anyone for a cocktail? We've plenty of ice."

"Please, Mr. Silver, snap out of it!" she begged, grabbing hold of him. But it was too late. As she spoke, another shoofa whipped past her father up above, spinning him around and off balance.

"No!" Madeline cried as the rope swung and her father fought for a terror-stricken moment to hold on—and then he too skidded over the edge of the crevasse, and followed the rope and his daughter, with Sebastian and Mesmer clinging tightly to her, down into the dark blue depths.

Down and down they fell, bouncing and sliding off

sheer icy surfaces, the air so cold around them it burned. The crevasse began to narrow—Madeline felt the ice walls draw closer. She remembered Sebastian's words. They would perish, painfully wedged in the bottom of this crevasse. She longed to see her mother and Rufus again. But she'd failed to keep her promise to her brother. She closed her eyes and waited for the crunch of landing and the end.

But it never came.

Instead the four travelers splashed down into a rushing flow of liquid ice and frozen rocks—they were numb instantly. They'd found the lethal river at the belly of the glacier.

Madeline lost Sebastian and Mesmer as they hit the water, so she nearly cried with relief when her father thrust his hand into hers as he washed past. They spun on through the churning, chaotic darkness, clinging to each other. Madeline felt her heart freezing within her. We're going to die like frozen fish, she thought. But just then, through her half-closed eyes, she saw something.

"Father," she said, forcing her frozen fingers to tighten on his hand. "Look—a light up ahead."

TWENTY-TWO

# The Prison

Elizabeth stormed into the Tullock mansion brimful of rage. The color was high in her cheeks, and her pale fists were clenched by her side. To Tullock, she was even more beautiful than ever. His face lit up. He raised a hand, and One-spike and Three-spike, who had marched in behind her, hammers at the ready, stepped away.

"You came," he said.

"What did you think I'd do?" Elizabeth responded. "Sit around playing solitaire?"

Aspid pushed herself up from her chair with several agonized puffs and wheezes.

"You must be so proud of your son," Elizabeth sneered at the old crone as she shuffled her way across the hall.

"Oh, I am. Very," Aspid replied. "And you could do better," she mumbled to Tullock as she passed him and headed up to her tower.

"Now where is *my* son?" Elizabeth demanded.

"Safe and well. Reveling in luxury," Tullock replied.

"So nice of him to visit." He motioned to an enormous wine rack crammed with dusty vintage bottles. "Come, sit with me for a while. Have some wine. Let's spend an evening enjoying the snow and ruminating on how much better things could be."

Elizabeth grabbed one of the bottles and threw it against the wall. The glass shattered, and the ruby-red contents splashed and dripped down over a stuffed owl.

"That bottle was priceless," Tullock huffed.

"It isn't anymore," Elizabeth retorted. "Now, once more, where is he?"

"It's your passion that stirs me." Tullock smiled charmingly again. "You really are wasted on that groveling idiot."

"You're nothing compared to Philip."

Tullock's nostrils flared. "Tread carefully now, Elizabeth," he growled, his lip curling. "Go easy this evening. Think. You have a chance to leave that festering, turnip-riddled world behind—"

"A world that *you* created," Elizabeth flared up.

"—and join me here," Tullock continued, "in opulence and splendor. Even your husband has deserted. Take your chance now. You want all this, admit it. Join me at last."

Elizabeth glowered. "Never!"

She watched something shift in Tullock's strong features. Something she hadn't seen before.

"Loyalty. I admire it. Though maybe it's time we tested it," he said coldly. "You could have everything. You really could." Tullock nodded to the two Hammer Squad members. They stepped forward and grabbed Elizabeth's arms. "But I suppose I knew it would come to this," Tullock went on. "The prison. I'll be along shortly." As Elizabeth was dragged away he added, "And tomorrow your house and any remaining fans, those pathetic symbols of defiance, will be firewood!"

"Our spirit isn't inside that house. It's here!" Elizabeth said, clamping her fist to her chest.

"Face it—the Breeze family is finished." Tullock gave a dismissive wave.

The prison, buried deep within the foundations of the Tullock mansion, was a vast pillared dungeon that had been carved out of the rock.

There were dozens of iron cages on chains hanging from the ceiling and they were all empty save one—which held a shivering Rufus.

He gripped the bars of his cage and looked around the vast enclosure with awe and a growing sense of unease. He had been trying to sleep, the adventures of the night before having sapped his strength, but his surroundings were hardly conducive.

There were various nasty-looking racks, stocks and other monstrous instruments around the edges of the dungeon, and in the middle a huge, darkly deep hole fell away to sea level. Rufus could hear the water surging and lapping at the bottom.

Even more unsettling, suspended vertically in space over the hole was the biggest sheet of ice Rufus had ever seen. It was as though it had been lifted in one piece from a frozen lake. The surface rippled with blue and gray echoes as some hurried activity went on behind it. Rufus heard the clang of metallic boots on stone and shuffled around inside his cage to see One-spike and Three-spike dragging . . . oh no . . . his mother to the rock floor below him. His heart sank. The guards flung her down and retreated back up the stone staircase, melting into darkness.

"Mother!" Rufus called out. His voice reverberated around the walls.

Elizabeth's face snapped upward. "Rufus! You're alive!"

"You shouldn't have come," Rufus went on. "You should have stayed with the house."

"Nonsense," his mother said.

But Rufus felt sick—he had failed his father, left the Breeze house unprotected and drawn his mother into danger. Yet how relieved he was too, not to be alone in this dungeon anymore. He tried to look brave for his mother's sake. "Hey, room with a view," he said, spreading his arms wide.

A moment later Rufus's cage was lowered. The door sprang open and he stepped out. His mother hugged him close.

"This, apparently, is a prison," Rufus said, trying to sound nonchalant.

"So I heard," his mother replied shakily. "What do you think he's got planned?"

The expansive sheet of ice hanging in front of them gave a sudden crack.

"I think we're about to find out," Rufus said as the ice sheet was released.

With a slow, weighty tumble it fell toward the depths of the cave's giant hole, shattering into thousands of fragments as it hit the rocks and icebergs floating in the water at the bottom. The sight that was now revealed made Rufus frown with bemusement.

# TWENTY-THREE

# The Balance of Power

Suspended from the dungeon's ceiling, hanging over the great hole in the floor, was a giant set of scales—a gargantuan seesaw with a massive tray at each end, both level at that moment. On one of the huge trays was a full-size model of the Breeze house, carved in ice. And on the other balanced at least thirty people. They were all wearing masks that had been painted to look like . . . his father, Rufus realized. This couldn't be good!

His mother gasped. "Who would dream up something like this? And why?"

Rufus pointed to a rock balcony high above the center point of the scales. Tullock stood there, staring down at them, his dark eyes burning hot.

"I don't usually go to these elaborate lengths," he called down. "Most people break or swear loyalty to me after a thumbscrew or two. But I figured you'd both be tougher nuts to crack."

"What *is* all this?" Rufus called back.

"Let's be clear. We don't have to go through with it," Tullock replied. "Just say the word, Elizabeth, and you can live here happily with me. I'm sure we can find something worthwhile for the boy to do too."

"I'll never work for you!" Rufus cried as his mother restrained him.

"That's what they all say to begin with," Tullock sneered. He paused and then turned the emotional thumbscrew tighter. "Windy won't be coming back, by the way, if that makes your decision any easier."

"You're full of hot air, Tullock," Rufus yelled. "My father *will* return!"

"Hmm, let's just say I know where he's headed and wheels are in motion to ensure his downfall if he even gets that far," Tullock said, smiling nastily.

Rufus heard his mother give a small, frightened gasp. Suddenly he felt sick with the hopelessness of the situation.

"But you two needn't suffer . . . Elizabeth?" Tullock wheedled.

"And if my mother doesn't say the word?" Rufus demanded.

"In a moment I will ignite a series of burners under your ice house," Tullock said. "As the sculpture melts, and the water runs away, it will become lighter. It won't be long before your beloved father, here denoted by a group of 'volunteers,' will be heavier. And when the tray holding them drops to its lowest point, it will tip and they will simply slide off and all the poor Philip Breezes will drop down into the sea at the bottom of my dungeon."

Rufus walked over to the edge of the hole and peered down into the churning surf.

"And I have cephalopods!" Tullock bellowed insanely.

"How unfortunate for you," Rufus quipped.

But Tullock smiled. "Giant cold-water octopuses. They like nothing more than to stab unfortunate Pinrutians with their beaks, poison them and then suck out their innards. It's quite a spectacle."

Sure enough, thick tentacles flickered in the waves below. Rufus shuddered. His mother put her face in her hands.

"So it is your job to save your home and Windy," Tullock said, his tone suddenly very serious.

A hole opened up in the roof of the cave above Rufus and his mother, and a deluge of snow started to fall from it onto their heads.

"If you throw snowballs at your house, they will stick and keep the weight constant," Tullock said. "Of course, it will be endlessly exhausting, but believe me, there's no shortage of snow. I'm lighting the burners now."

Rufus saw an orange glow appear beneath the ice

house, and almost instantly water began to trickle from the sculpture, pool on the rim of its copper tray, then drip away. The house rose, barely an inch, but it rose. The tray of people dipped by the same amount. Frantically, Rufus scooped up a handful of snow and packed it tight. He hurled the snowball at the house sculpture, where it stuck to an icy windowpane. The house lowered again slightly.

"This is crazy," his mother yelled angrily.

"We won't give in to you, Tullock!" Rufus added.

"There is a bellpull behind you," Tullock said, pointing to a length of rope that dangled down behind Elizabeth. "If you change your minds, just give it a tug. But for now I shall leave you to your endeavors. I have my own chores to attend to. Not that destroying your *actual* house is a chore—more of a fun day out." With a satisfied grunt, Tullock turned on his heel and walked out of sight.

"This is madness," Elizabeth said as she watched Rufus throw another snowball at the ice sculpture and bent to pack her own.

"Well, he is mad," Rufus said, gathering more snow. If he could just keep this up long enough to think, if they stayed calm . . .

He looked over at the balancing people. A sea of Philip Breezes stared back at him.

"Take off those ridiculous masks!" he called.

One by one the people removed them. They were mostly older men and women, a grubby-looking bunch, thin and tired—obviously dragged in from the fields. But asking them to remove their masks had been a mistake. They had also acted as blindfolds, and now, as the men and women looked around at their surroundings, terror began to spread.

The wild movements of the trapped villagers made the giant set of scales shift and groan.

"Please, don't panic!" Rufus called up. "You'll bring the whole thing down!"

The people stopped suddenly, frozen in fear.

"I'm thinking of a way to get you out of there!"

"Oh, those poor people," his mother almost sobbed. "They didn't deserve to be made part of this. We have to stop it." She took a step toward the bellpull.

"Mother—no," Rufus snapped. "He won't bargain. We'd end up captives here forever and these people would probably be fed to the octopuses anyway. They're too old for the fields; I bet this is just Tullock 'retiring' them." Rufus packed up another snowball and hurled it at the dripping ice house. It stuck to the front door with a wet thud. "We need to think of a way to get us and them out of here."

"How?" his mother asked.

Rufus was looking around desperately as he scooped up another snowball. Suddenly he noticed something about the pivot point at the center of the giant scales.

"Now, there's a rather crude use for a centripetal rosehub," he said.

# TWENTY-FOUR

# A Bizarre Border House

Unusually, the western edge of the Great Glacier ended abruptly in a massive cliff face of jagged ice, pitted with grubby rock debris. At the base of it was a small arched opening, and the glacier river emerged from this into the snowy plain, frothing with energy.

Madeline had never been so grateful to look up at a blizzardy sky in her life. As the water shallowed and slowed, Madeline and her father were able at last to scramble to the riverbank and heave themselves out. Sebastian followed with Mesmer. They were all shaking, not only with the cold, but with shock at the nature of their dramatic passage across and through the Great Glacier. But they'd made it, and the sight that now greeted them was so extraordinary that those thoughts quickly dissolved. Madeline's jaw dropped open.

Sebastian lifted a soggy boot from crisp snow, swung it forward and put it down on . . . dry, sun-baked dirt. This was the western Pinrut border. A hard, dividing line. Snow on one side . . . dazzling sunshine on the other. With a grin, Sebastian took another step, and the snow fell in a sheer wall behind him. The sun shone brightly, and rolling dusty hills with patches of yellow grass lay before him. The river that gushed forth from the base of the glacier dried to a mere trickle in the middle distance. Exotic cactuses punctuated the parched brown landscape around it.

"Ah! Everything's thawing out nicely!" Sebastian exclaimed. At his feet, Mesmer shook the remaining water from his coat and let out a long, extravagant yawn.

"Now, this is really quite unusual," Madeline's father muttered as he also stepped clear of the snow.

"I told you the weather was a little mixed up around these parts," Sebastian said. His hat was starting to steam as the water evaporated from it rapidly.

Philip turned his face toward the sun's warmth. "It's been so long." His voice was thick with emotion.

Madeline hung back for a moment though—these strange localized extremities of weather were more than unusual or mixed up. They were downright worrying, and she felt sure there must be an explanation. But as she had no idea what it was, she decided she might as well follow the others.

As she took a step into sunshine for the first time in her life, Madeline slapped her hands over her eyes. "Father, it's so bright."

Sebastian rummaged in his satchel and pulled out a pair of bizarre-looking sunglasses. They had big bronze frames and lenses of thick brown glass.

"Miraculous precision instruments to diminish the sun's luminosity," he exclaimed as he gave them to Madeline. "You may borrow them at no cost."

Madeline looked at the crude glasses warily. But she figured they were better than nothing and took them all the same.

"That's easier," she admitted.

She pushed her already nearly dry hair away from her face, pulled off her cloak and looked about her. It was so beautiful she could hardly breathe, all the bright colors and a heat that seemed to wrap itself around her like the thickest blanket ever. She had never felt this warm in her life before . . . Actually, she was extremely warm, hot even, sweating. What she needed right now was, what? Well, a breeze or something or, she laughed to herself in delight—a fan! Reverently, she drew the fan made of feathers from her pocket, opened it out and slowly wafted it toward her face the way she had playacted so many times before. The rush of cool air was bliss. Ah, so much to tell Rufus! Remembering her sensible brother, she took another, more focused look around as she flapped the fan, and noticed a strange structure that lay across the dividing line between snow and sun to their right. "What a peculiar building," she said.

The border house was made up of two very distinct halves. On the snowy side it was built from thick stone with a thatched roof and small, deep-set windows. On the sunny side it was constructed out of wooden slats with red canvas awnings over large windows. Straddling the two sides was a single door, one half ice-covered and the other bleached and sun-baked.

And perched on the edge of a snow-covered chimney pot on the thatched half of the roof was a giant raven just like the one that had flown over them on the glacier. It peered down at Madeline with piercing eyes, and she didn't like it. She didn't like it at all.

But her father and Sebastian didn't seem that interested in the house.

"Well, we made it!" Sebastian was exclaiming, laughing heartily and ruffling Mesmer's ears, much to Mesmer's apparent disgust. "Woo-hoo! What a rush coming down through that glacier, eh? The *only* way to travel. And here we are! Tresedira awaits our fans—thataway. Yes, sir. Won't be long now!"

Madeline saw her father's face fall as the same horrible realization hit her, with a thump. She turned to Sebastian with a stony expression.

"What?" he asked innocently.

"The endeavors of a lifetime . . . ," her father was murmuring mournfully.

"The whole reason we're making this trip—they're

still up on that glacier!" Madeline said furiously. "And basically it's all thanks to you, Mr. Silver! We should never have gone that way in the first place." Madeline sank to the dusty ground dejectedly. What could she say or do to help her father now?

"Ah. Good point," Sebastian muttered sheepishly. "And poor Turnip. He doesn't have a thing to eat; I have the bag of turnips here . . ."

"What? Of course!" Madeline leaped back up, propelled by a new spark of hope. "If you've still got them, do you think Turnip might have . . . ?" She spun around and peered upward. "Look, Father!" she exclaimed. Madeline pointed through the thick soup of snowflakes to the top of the glacier's terminal face. She stepped back into the falling snow with a shiver and looked up again, her heart thumping in her throat. Flakes settled on her still sun-warmed nose and melted instantly. The others joined her.

She heard her father gasp.

Right on the very edge of the glacier was Turnip, trotting back and forth and sniffing the air eagerly. He was so far up that he was only just visible.

"Guess he ran out of turnips and came looking for more," Madeline said under her breath. "Oh, he's so close to the edge." She chewed on the nail of her little finger anxiously.

The horse was skidding now, sending chunks of ice

over the cliff. Sebastian turned away. "O lamentable day! Our fortune is slipping through our unfortunate fingers! I can't look."

"He's going," Madeline's father said, clenching his hands into tight fists.

And sure enough, with a final, clumsy twist, then skid, the unfortunate animal simply dropped off the edge of the cliff. With a groan the unwieldy sled followed. "My fans," Philip wailed as he shut his eyes. Mesmer howled in unison. All Madeline could think of was poor Turnip.

The fans that Madeline and her father had tied to the sled to help its progress over the ice were the last things to fall off the edge of the glacier. Madeline could hear their frantic huffs, clicks and whirrs even from so far away as the air whistled through them while they fell. But as Madeline watched in horror, it began to seem to her that the horse's descent was slowing. How could that be? Was she so desperate to see the horse and sled safe that she was imagining it? Or . . . was it the fans? As the machines fell, their blades were turning faster and faster. They were trying to fly. And because there were so many of them, so securely attached, the horse and sled were slowing to a floating descent. Mesmer ceased his howl and put his head to one side with a quizzical yelp as a lone fan made of feathers escaped from the sled and fluttered down behind it like an exotic bird searching for its mate in Madeline's hand.

It wasn't pretty to look at—Turnip was now twisted sideways in a tangle of strings, and the sled dangled like some misshapen pendulum—but there would be no explosive landing.

The peculiar flying bundle came to a jangled but safe halt on the snow-sun border about thirty feet from where a speechless Madeline was standing. Snowflakes instantly began to settle on the horse's rear legs while the hot sunshine drew a sweat from his brow.

Madeline ran over and started to untangle poor Turnip. Mesmer, too, pulled at the bird's nest of fishing line with his teeth.

"Does somebody else want to help me?" Madeline asked.

Sebastian and her father both opened their eyes, and their jaws dropped.

"Your clever fans took the heat out of Turnip's tumble, Father," Madeline explained with delight as the two men bounded over. Philip patted the contents of the sled. Miraculously, all seemed to be well. In fact the monkey fan was still straining excitedly at its leash until, red eyes aglow, its spinning leather tail bopped Mesmer on the nose and Madeline switched it off.

As the wild-eyed Turnip was loosened, Sebastian did a happy little jig on the spot.

"So a slightly unorthodox journey so far," he conceded. Madeline and Mesmer exchanged disbelieving glances at this understatement. "But it looks as though we're back on track!"

Just as Sebastian finished speaking, the door of the border house flew open to reveal a hulking Hammer guard.

"Oh no," Madeline groaned.

He pointed at the mangled sled and its contents with a large, shining hammer.

"I have orders to impound your cart and contents," he growled. Without another word he snatched Turnip's reins and tied him to a metal ring set in the stonework of the snowy side of the border house. Then he motioned for the others to follow him inside.

# TWENTY-FIVE

# Elizabeth's Anguish

Rufus continued to hurl snowballs at the melting sculpture of his home, his mind ticking over frantically. His mother was doing her best too, but her aim wasn't as good as his. And despite their best efforts, the house was melting faster than they could compensate for anyway. Things were not looking good. The people on the giant scales' tray were sinking. It wouldn't be long now before they were lost to the thrashing creatures in the depths below. But so far he'd had only one idea—having spotted the centripetal rose-hub—and it was very risky. He thought of Madeline—that wouldn't stop her, would it?

"Mother, I'm going to have to stop for a few moments," Rufus said breathlessly. "Can you manage?"

Elizabeth panted. "I'll do my best."

Rufus packed a jumbo-sized snowball and lobbed it with both hands up in the air. It soared in a lazy arc and landed on the ice-house chimney. The scales tipped and the house lowered somewhat. As the people rose, there was a ragged cheer.

Immediately, Rufus turned and started to scale the cliff wall next to the bellpull. He clambered up about twenty feet and pulled a sharp knife from his toolbelt. "What are you doing, Rufus?" his mother called as she threw a snowball and missed. The people on the scales let out a small groan.

Rufus cut through the bellpull with a single decisive swipe, then clambered back down and gathered up the length of rope.

"I'm tipping the scales in our favor."

He pulled his claw hammer from his belt and lashed it to one end of the rope. In only the short time it had taken him to do all this the doors and windows carved in the ice house had already melted away. The people were starting to plunge downward.

"We're sinking!" cried out one.

"The octopuses are ready for us!" cried another.

"This is awful," Elizabeth said, running her frozen hands through her hair.

Rufus was whirling the hammer on the rope about his head now, building up momentum. With a final heave he let go, and the claw hammer sailed through the air and dug itself into the mound of ice with a pulpy squelch. The tray instantly dropped slightly and the Pinrutians rose. Rufus pulled on the rope with one hand to make sure the hammer was well embedded—the tray bobbed but the hammer didn't shift—and with the other he twisted his sun-shaped cuff links for luck. His stomach was churning, but he knew he had to try it.

"I hope you're not thinking of . . . ," his mother started.

She did not have time to finish as Rufus launched himself over the pit.

"Rufus, no!"

He was dangling in thin air now. His weight pulled the slush-filled tray down farther, and the people on the other side of the scales were lifted accordingly. They cheered. It was a rather feeble cheer, tempered by years of fatigue, but a cheer all the same.

"Be careful!" Rufus heard his mother call out.

Slowly Rufus heaved himself up the rope so that he was standing on the scales' tray. He yanked the claw hammer from the ice, wound the rope into a coil and attached it to his toolbelt. Then he began to walk along the arm that connected to the pivot point halfway between the two trays.

The arm was narrow—Rufus felt like a tightrope walker. Although his movements were steady, his mouth was dry and his palms were slick with cold sweat. As he moved along the arm, inevitably the ice house started to rise and the people to fall again. His mother could hardly watch.

"We're going to drop!" cried one of the trapped women, wringing her reddened hands.

A giant white tentacle snaked up from the water below and flicked at the bottom of the now dangerously low tray. Any minute it would surely tip.

"Everyone crouch down and hold on!" Rufus yelled as he reached the central pivot point and pulled a screwdriver from his toolbelt. He began to tinker with the centripetal rose-hub that was embedded there. In the next moment the arm with the huddled Pinrutians on the end of it was rising again, independent of the other tray. The adjusted mechanism that Rufus had created made a robust clunking noise as it hoisted.

"I told you these centripetal rose-hubs were pretty amazing!" Rufus called to his mother with relief. She smiled at him proudly, but he saw her shiver too in the still falling snow. He had to hurry.

When the arm was almost vertical, it stopped, the tray level with Tullock's stone balcony.

"Keep to the shadows and you might escape," Rufus hissed upward. "Go!"

As the villagers hopped onto the balcony and disappeared into the darkness, they called their thanks.

"You go too, Rufus. Climb up and get away. I'll be all right," his mother cried out.

But Rufus was trying to lever the centripetal rose-hub out of the pivot with the handle of a wrench. "First I'm going to extract this and then we're *both* getting out of here, Mother, and back to the house to get the defenses working," Rufus replied.

Just then the centripetal rose-hub fell free. It was about the size of a biscuit barrel, and its heart-shaped pieces glinted attractively. Rufus caught it and hooked it onto his toolbelt.

But its release was followed almost instantly by a sickening, grinding noise. Rufus realized too late what he had done. The rose-hub had not merely been part of the scale's pivot mechanism—apparently it had been holding the whole contraption together. Now that it was gone, the scales were beginning to break apart. Rufus met his mother's gaze. She was shaking her head in disbelief and horror.

Another part of the scales dropped away beneath him. Rufus had only a moment to feel angry at himself for acting so rashly, to hope the rest of his scattered family would be all right. Then, with a crunching noise, the part on which he was standing broke off and he plummeted down toward the surging, tentacled waters below. As he fell, he thought, Tullock caused this. Then he hit the water. So Rufus did not see his mother's eyes go wide with anguish as she stared down at the spreading circle of white foam where her son had disappeared and dived in after him.

## TWENTY-SIX

# Madeline's Bold Plan

The interior of the border house was just as curious as the exterior. The snowy side was furnished with rugs, blankets and thick curtains. The sunny side had bare floorboards and a hammock—and a huge man wearing sandals and decorative light armor swaying in it. A heavy-looking saber hung by his side. He was obviously a guard, but not one of Tullock's Hammer Squad. Madeline, her father and Sebastian were tied to rings in the wall on the cold side. Mesmer was also tied up, though there was enough rope that he could lie down, with his chin resting despondently on his blue paws.

"Well, who could have foreseen this? Hmm?" Sebastian mused.

Madeline watched the massive Hammer guard as he stared out the window at the snow, tapping his hammer on the stone floor.

"So what are you going to do with us, tin-head?" she

asked. Normally in circumstances like these, she would have been chewing on her fingernail, but it was tied behind her back.

"There are more Hammer Squad members on the way from Pinrut," the guard replied, his voice hollow. "They will escort you back to be sentenced by the Tullock family for running out on a debt."

Sebastian looked disturbed. "Um, I don't actually come from Pinrut," he ventured. "Thus, perhaps the dog and I can go free? I mean, I hope you don't think we were conspiring alongside these two . . . ragamuffins—we've only just met."

Madeline rolled her eyes. She wasn't surprised to learn that their trickster traveling companion was also well versed in the art of double-crossing self-preservation.

The Hammer guard approached Sebastian and leaned his hideous helmet with the bulbous glass eyes over him.

"Tullock is a very fair, inclusive ruler, come one, come all," he said. "So whatever fate befalls these two will be visited upon you also."

"Well, it's nice to be wanted," Sebastian replied dejectedly.

The guard moved back toward the window as Madeline narrowed her eyes at Sebastian.

"Sorry," Sebastian said, red-faced. "I had to try." But Madeline was too busy hatching a plan to dwell on it.

Mr. Silver's satchel was still on his shoulder, and it was digging into her side. And she could hear Turnip snuffling on the other side of the wall. As she surreptitiously worked her fingers into the bag and around a turnip, she spoke to the guard in the hammock on the hot side of the border house.

"We were heading into the sunshine to sell fans," she said brightly.

At her side, her father gave a despondent sigh. The guard observed her lazily. "Virtuous plan," he said, wiping the sweat from his brow with the back of his thumb.

Sebastian gave Madeline an admiring nod.

"Even in these conditions you're trying for a sale—a girl after my own heart," he whispered.

"No, Mr. Silver," Madeline replied coldly. "That's not what I'm trying to do at all."

"Don't be modest," Sebastian muttered. "I'm impressed. You could have a big sale here."

"And what would be the point of that?" Madeline whispered.

"Money," Sebastian replied. "Moolah, spondoolies."

"Money's no good if we're dead," Madeline hissed fiercely.

"Stop whispering!" the Hammer guard growled.

"So you wouldn't keep us from selling our fans then?" Madeline went on quickly, turning back to the man in the hammock.

He shrugged. "Not at all—if you were in my domain. But it looks like you're stuck in the cold with old bucketface there. So bad luck."

That was all Madeline needed to know. With a flick of her wrist, she threw the turnip she had worked loose across the room and out of the window on the hot side of the border house.

"What the . . . ?" the Hammer guard spluttered. Madeline heard a snort of excitement from the other side of the wall as Turnip spotted the vegetable lying in the sun-baked dust. Then he began to pull toward it. He heaved, he whinnied. The wall behind Madeline groaned . . . and then gave way. Turnip galloped across the border, dragging the battered sled, the fans and a large chunk of wall, with Madeline and her companions still tied to it.

The Hammer guard lunged after them, but with a sudden surge of energy the hot-side guard leaped from his hammock and drew his saber. The blade flashed in the sun as he waved it through the doorway.

"Hey, hey, back on your side, pot-chops," he said, his voice now thick with authority as he went to untie Madeline first.

Helplessly, the Hammer guard took a step backward into snow. Madeline stuck her tongue out at him gleefully, then patted Turnip's sun-warmed nose as he munched contentedly.

"Do you have a cart we can borrow?" she asked the hot-side guard. "In return for a fabulous fan perhaps?"

"Your daughter is most impressive," Sebastian said as the guard agreed to a deal.

Philip began to unload his precious fans from the broken sled.

# TWENTY-SEVEN

# Fans on Trial

Madeline, her father and Sebastian dumped their cloaks, coats and scarves on the cart as soon as they left the border house, but they were still pink-faced and uncomfortably hot as they led Turnip up a sharp incline onto a rocky ridge. Madeline flapped frantically at her face with her feather fan while Sebastian and Mesmer shared the other.

At the top of the ridge they all stopped to catch their breath—and stared. Before them was a startling view. Stretching off endlessly to the west were miles and miles of arid desert. The undulating dunes shimmered in the heat, their molten haze almost blinding. And at last, in the distance, they saw what looked like a town shimmering on the horizon.

"Behold—Tresedira!" Sebastian exclaimed.

"It actually exists," Madeline said softly.

"Of course it exists!" Sebastian blustered. "What—

did you think I was some madman luring you into the middle of nowhere only to rob you or get you lost?"

"Well, you haven't exactly been Mr. Reliable so far . . . ," Madeline couldn't help retorting.

"I can't believe I'm hearing this!" Sebastian exclaimed indignantly. "I'm the man to have in your corner! Mesmer, tell them!"

Mesmer let out a low whine and suddenly became very interested in sniffing a little lizard sitting on a rock.

"Mr. Silver, calm down." Madeline had a feeling Sebastian was very practiced in long-winded wounded-pride rants. If she didn't stop him now, who knew how long they'd be here. "You mustn't get excited in this heat. And I admit . . . you did lead us to Tresedira, as promised."

Sebastian plucked a yellow handkerchief from a pocket and mopped his brow in an injured fashion.

Madeline turned to her father. He was gazing dreamily toward Tresedira with a slight smile on his face. It seemed even Mr. Silver's shrill rants had not disturbed his reverie.

Sebastian saw it too, and he stuffed his handkerchief back in his pocket and gave the fanmaker a dazzling smile. Clearly he was not one to hold grudges.

"Our fortune awaits in Tresedira!" he called as he set off down the first dune. "A geyser of gold!"

"Well, we're not there yet," Madeline's father cautioned suddenly. He squinted down at the shadeless, sandy plains. "It's like a furnace out there. I doubt we have enough water to make it to Tresedira unless we keep cool."

"Why don't we wear the perambulator fans, Father?" Madeline suggested.

"Now, why didn't I think of that?" Philip replied.

Sebastian watched with interest as Mr. Breeze pulled one of his more bizarre-looking contraptions from the back of the cart. He strapped the ornate metal framework to his chest and tied its two leather loops around his thighs. The loops were attached to wires, which were hooked to racks of teeth on the chest unit, which drove a cog, which spun the fan blades. The blades atop the chest unit faced Philip's face; the two on the side, his body.

"This one looks kind of kooky," Sebastian mused.

"My father's fans are *not* kooky," Madeline said defiantly. "They're beautiful and clever. They're brilliant. Why, this fan cools you with every step you take."

"Let's see it in action then," Sebastian urged.

"Er . . . ," Philip said. He didn't move a muscle. Madeline gave her little finger a chew.

"Oh, oh, oh! I get it! This must be the first time in a long while you've used one of your fans for real in the sun, correct?" Sebastian crowed. "BIG moment! Wow."

"Ha! Don't be ridiculous. All my fans have been fully tested," Philip replied nervously.

"Where? In a blizzard? On an ice floe?"

Madeline surreptitiously crossed her fingers as her father took a small, tentative step. The wire attached to his leading leg tightened and the blades on the chest box, which were a few inches under his chin, turned one revolution. He felt a whisper of relief from the wilting temperature. Encouraged by this, he took another step, then another. Faster and faster—the blades began spinning. Philip's straw-colored hair lifted in the cool breeze.

"It works!" he cried. "Er, just like I knew it did."

Madeline breathed a sigh of relief. "I'll get two more out of the cart."

Mesmer let out a bad-tempered growl.

"Oops! Sorry, Mesmer, did we forget you?"

Soon Mesmer and Turnip were also proudly sporting special pet-edition perambulator fans of their own, lashed to their chests. Mesmer looked more than a little dubious about his.

Within minutes Madeline and her father, Sebastian, Mesmer and Turnip were striding down onto the scalding hot sands that led to Tresedira. The syncopated rhythm of the chattering machines provided a musical backdrop for them to march by.

Madeline couldn't help smiling as she turned toward

Tresedira and felt the refreshing breeze on her face and her long hair streaming out behind her. This was what fans were for. This was the sunny but breezy life her father had talked about.

Maybe everything was going to be all right.

# TWENTY-EIGHT

# An Underwater Tussle

The shock of the cold seawater brought Rufus to his senses. He opened his eyes to discover he was a long way below the surface. His heavy mop of hair fanned out around his face like a golden halo. He felt in one piece, but a quick glance around made him shudder. Thick, opalescent tentacles with ugly blue veins thrashed all about him, and he caught a glimpse of several large, cruel-looking beaks and the glowing, gelatinous eyes above them, looming through the foam-filled water.

His head began to buzz. He had to get to the surface and breathe, but before he could move, a line of soft but incredibly strong suckers attached themselves to his body. A tentacle thicker than his waist began to wrap itself around him, tighter and tighter. Rufus felt what little breath he had left leave him like toothpaste being squeezed out of a tube. All was lost—surely. His strength was fading, his mind filling with confused images—beautiful fans made of falling snow. He thought of his sister.

And from deep inside him a spark of vitality returned. With an awkward twist of his arm he plucked a small saw from his toolbelt and hacked into the rubbery white limb.

The octopus arm flailed. It tossed Rufus aside and upward, and as he broke the surface, he drew in a long desperate breath before falling back into the churning water.

Then, again amidst the chaos of the crowded, hungry octopuses, something terrible caught his attention—a tentacle-wrapped figure in green with billowing red hair . . . being drawn toward a waiting beak. It was his mother! She must have dived in after him. Air bubbles were streaming weakly from her mouth. Her eyes were closed and her face was pale. The octopus beak parted.

Rufus stared into its foul mouth and felt rage coursing through his blood. He darted toward the sandy seabed and something shiny resting on it. He was in luck. It was a shard of metal, as long as Rufus was tall, part of one of the arms from Tullock's giant set of scales. Rufus grabbed the makeshift weapon from the seabed and kicked his way upward as hard as he could.

As a strand of his mother's hair came close enough to the dreaded beak to float into it, as the last air bubble left her lips, he thrust the metal shard into the rubbery underbelly of the octopus.

There was a wild, watery screech as the creature lashed

out, knocking Rufus sideways. Black ink started to flood the water. But before it became totally opaque, Rufus spotted his mother drifting slowly downward like a discarded doll. He kicked toward her, then swam for the surface, dragging his mother with him.

The octopuses were fighting over the body of the dying octopus now, and he had to be careful not to get caught up in the chaos. Tentacles knotted and broke the water's surface. Fountains of dark blood spattered onto a crisp white iceberg, staining it blue like an angry bruise.

The air felt sweet as he gasped to fill his lungs. He glanced at his mother's ashen face and a feeling of dread swept over him. But then she started to cough, and he watched her gulp in air and open her eyes. Rufus smiled with relief and took another deep breath.

The rock walls around them were too sheer to climb, but the sea had to be entering the giant well from somewhere. Rufus just needed to find out where that was before the octopuses finished with one another and started to wonder where their tasty human morsels had gone.

An hour later Rufus and his mother pulled themselves up onto rocks at the base of a cliff, at the point where a narrow path dotted with stone steps led up toward the Tullock mansion. The building was so immense that

Rufus had a dizzying, irrational feeling that the whole edifice was going to topple down on him suddenly. The snow was falling, as heavy as ever, the flakes dissolving as they struck the salt water. It had been quite a search to find the narrow hole in the rock that led out into the open sea, and they were painfully cold.

"If we hurry through the forest, we may be able to get home before the Hammer Squad," he urged, straightening his clothes. "Are you all right, Mother?" he added, noticing that she was shaking violently.

"Just tired and need to warm my blood," Elizabeth replied, rubbing the backs of her arms vigorously. "I'll be fine."

"It won't take them long to realize we're all gone," Rufus said. "Hopefully they'll think we were eaten, but they'll be looking for us too. The sooner we get back home the better . . ."

Rufus and his mother stuck to the gray shadows provided by the biggest trees in the Reffinock forest. For once Rufus was grateful to the falling snow for rapidly covering their tracks.

He was hopeful too—if they could just get back to the house before Tullock's guards struck, he could patch up the defenses pretty quickly with the centripetal rosehub Tullock had so kindly supplied. Then all they had to do was await Father's triumphant return as planned.

He had decided not to believe Tullock's taunts about that.

But as they approached the square where they lived, skirting the town's other gray houses carefully, their hopes were crushed by what they saw. Their house was already gone.

# TWENTY-NINE

# Sebastian's Story

After a long, hot day trudging under a blazing sun, the travelers arrived gratefully at a small shining pool of water in the middle of the desert. Palm trees leaned in toward each other over the pool, like the bones of a giant rib cage.

The perambulator fans had worked well all day, but everyone welcomed the chance to stop and remove them. Things still seemed so new to Madeline: the rich blue of the sky, the way the sunlight glinted off surfaces, the warm air and the cool breeze of the fans against it. Her senses were being overloaded, but she tried to absorb it all nonetheless. She wanted to be able to share every detail with her brother when she saw him again.

The surface of the water sparkled as golden fish swam to and fro with lazy flicks of their tails. The atmosphere was thick with humidity and the birds seemed to coast from one point to another on warm air currents alone, too weary with heat to beat their wings.

Mesmer bounded over to the edge of the pool and began to drink deeply, his lapping tongue sending out rhythmic waves. Madeline unhooked Turnip from the cart, and the horse also trotted over to the water and drank, his heavy head bobbing happily next to Mesmer's blue furry face.

Sebastian heaved off his discolored boots, strode into the pool up to his shins and gave a contented sigh. He removed his hat with a flourish and pointed down at his feet.

"Ah, this is the feeling we are selling, Mr. Breeze," he said. "Raucous relief! A priceless pause from perspiration! Sanctuary from that sizzling sun!" Sebastian jabbed an accusing finger at the shimmering orange orb that was now sinking behind the treetops far to the west.

Madeline and her father had also removed their boots, and now they sat down on a large rock a little distance from Sebastian, dangling their toes in the water. Madeline plopped a pretty little glass fan in the shape of a swan into the pool. It bobbed to the surface and began to draw water up its neck with a transparent pump. Then it breezed a fine, cooling mist over them from its beak as it circled, its feet paddling urgently. Madeline's father examined the toes that had been exposed by his one split boot gingerly—first frostbitten, now sunburned!

"He talks a lot, doesn't he?" Madeline said, glancing over at Sebastian.

"Some people do their thinking that way," Philip replied distractedly. "And some people do it instead of thinking."

Madeline swung her feet awkwardly in the water, sending out ripples that transformed the golden fish into jagged displays of abstract color. "I've been thinking about Rufus and Mother," she admitted.

"Sunshine, me too," Philip said as he pushed a stray lock of hair from her shiny face. "But they've got my father's brilliant defenses and the thought of our gold-laden return to keep them going—and we're so nearly there." He indicated Tresedira, shimmering on the horizon, much closer now. "It'll be easy from here on in."

"Of course." Madeline smiled and tried to let her father's blind optimism reassure her, and so him. But a vague sense of unease still fluttered inside her.

Sebastian splashed over to them and seated himself with a theatrical sigh on the opposite side of the rock.

Mesmer hopped up beside him and settled down for a satisfying chew on a piece of bark.

A restful hush descended on the travelers for a few minutes.

"So where do you come from, Sebastian?" Madeline's father asked finally when the silence started to hang heavy in the air.

"It's not where we come from that's important, Philip, but where we're going," Sebastian replied.

"But where we come from shapes where we're going," Madeline frowned.

Sebastian laughed. "My apologies. I had forgotten I was traveling with two philosophers."

"You can't always have been on your own and on the move, Mr. Silver," Madeline tried, her curiosity awakened. "Don't you have any family?"

"No," Sebastian replied. "Except Mesmer. But we make the perfect partnership—I've got the looks and he's got the brains. Other than that it's a case of . . . dumped on a doorstep as a baby, brought up in a poorhouse. A tedious tale and lamentably lacking in originality, I'm afraid." His usual brash exterior seemed to dissolve momentarily. "But I've come a long way since then," he managed eventually.

"And that's why money is so important to you?" Madeline murmured. "At the expense of all else?"

"Sure! Money's honey." Sebastian brightened. "Can't dress like a prince with empty pockets now, can you?" He turned to look at Madeline and her father. "What else is there?" He gave a hollow laugh, then ruffled Mesmer's ears with gusto. The dog frowned. "Don't know about you two but I'm exhausted. Let's boil up some turnips and pitch camp! We'll hit Tresedira fresh tomorrow."

Madeline set to peeling vegetables thoughtfully, with many a glance in Sebastian's direction.

Later that night, Madeline was the only one still awake.

She watched a lone bird fly overhead. It let out a single sharp caw before sweeping away to the west. Her gaze drifted to Sebastian, who was propped up against one of the cartwheels, his hat pulled down over his eyes, asleep.

"Shoes are shoes, madam, no one specified for which feet, after all," he mumbled through shallow snores. "Ah, Elder Sourflood . . . of course I'll return with your tools . . . soon . . . soon . . ."

Now that they were so close to Tresedira, butterflies fluttered in her stomach. Had they been foolish to come on this trip with Sebastian Silver? She stroked the little leather ears of the monkey fan hovering above her for comfort. Its red eyes glowed warmly. Would things go well once they reached Tresedira? And even if they did, how would she and her father get back to Pinrut safely with the gold? And all the time they were away, how were Rufus and Mother faring? These thoughts tumbled around in her mind like stones being bounced along a riverbed as she finally fell asleep.

# The Genius of Clement Breeze

The Breeze house was truly gone. All that remained of it was Philip's underground workshop, now rapidly filling with snow. White flakes settled on polished metal surfaces and thickened like icing on a cake.

The Hammer Squad stood around the perimeter of the sunken room, still and silent. Rufus put a comforting arm around his shivering mother as they peered over the wall from across the square. His face was pale with disbelief.

They had obviously lost the race.

"They did it," Elizabeth whispered.

Rufus shook his head slowly. His father's workshop lay bare for all to see. It was as though the fanmaker's very soul had been put on public display.

Scratskin's black carriage rounded a corner and clattered along the street to stop by the hole where the Breeze house used to be. Tullock flung the door open and stormed over to One-spike. His mother's eyes gleamed from the shadows of the carriage.

Rufus and his mother were too far away to hear Tullock, but it was clear he was not happy.

Maybe it was because they'd started without him, Rufus thought bitterly. He watched One-spike shake his head and begin to gesticulate madly.

But Tullock only frowned, then spun around and pointed at another Hammer guard seemingly at random. He hissed something in his ear and the guard dropped his hammer and started to run, but Scratskin was too quick for him. He leaped from his seat atop the carriage, scooped up the fallen hammer and, with chilling accuracy, hefted it through the air to clout the fleeing guard in the back with a resounding clang. Elizabeth gave an involuntary gasp.

As Tullock delivered a final command out the carriage window, Scratskin lashed the unconscious guard to the luggage rack and took the reins once more. Tullock gave one last suspicious sweep of the area with glinting eyes that made Rufus shudder, and then the carriage swept away. The Hammer Squad dispersed, subdued.

Rufus was baffled. He'd expected Tullock to seem happier at achieving his long-term goal at last—the Breezes were homeless! Instead, it seemed the octopuses would be getting fed tonight after all, thought Rufus grimly, but by one of Tullock's own men . . .

When the area was clear, Rufus and his mother trudged over to the place where their house had once stood. Rufus's heart fell away into the pit before him. All his planning had been for nothing. Keeping the house safe had proved impossible. What would they do now, until his father returned—if he did?

In his gloom, Rufus did not notice Arabella emerging from her grubby house across the street. It was only when she hurried over to them and spoke that he saw her.

"Hey, you two," she said. Her voice was gentle. She threw two shabby cloaks around their still damp and now slightly icy shoulders.

"I can't believe he did it," Elizabeth mumbled.

"He didn't," Arabella replied. "Do you see any sign of demolition? No. Well then, follow me . . ."

Arabella led Rufus and his mother up a track deep into the dense Thorn Wood to the north of Pinrut. White hares darted in front of them, kicking up powdery snow with their muscular hind legs. Rufus noticed that on either side of the track were freshly broken branches and the snow underfoot had deep grooves in it. Something large had obviously been dragged along here in recent hours. But Arabella would tell him nothing. She only smiled.

Farther up the track, Rufus had his answer, however, for here Henry Bugle was guiding six skinny oxen, who in turn were dragging an extremely cumbersome and very curious-looking burden. It seemed to be a collection of windows, doors, roof tiles, wall panels and chimneys compressed higgledy-piggledy into a block, as if a giant had taken an ordinary house and . . . sat on it. Underneath this were wooden runners that allowed it to slide over the snow.

"Is that . . . our house?" Elizabeth asked. "How did . . ."

Arabella gave another mysterious smile.

Rufus ran his fingers over the strange object. It was about a tenth the size of their house. And the way it was folded was strangely beautiful, like one of the old-fashioned fans the Breeze family used to make early on in their trade. He would love to see the blueprints for this mechanism!

"I recognize the door except now it's divided into three," he said out loud.

"When your grandfather made this alteration to the house, he wanted it kept quiet," Henry explained. "Clement didn't want to raise suspicion or worry your father any more than he had to. He entrusted the secret to me, though, in case the worst happened. Once we removed some of your furniture, it turned in on itself like a dream."

"Make them well, make them beautifully," Rufus said almost to himself.

Arabella drew up beside him. "We'll take it a good long way up the track and then deep into the wood," she said.

She and Henry walked ahead to get the oxen to pull

harder, while Rufus fell back with his mother. She seemed oddly quiet. He spoke his thoughts aloud, hoping to lift her spirits.

"No wonder Tullock looked cross," he said. "The Hammer Squad must have told him the house was gone before they got there and he thought they were lying." Rufus chuckled for a moment, but then a darker thought struck him. "Mind you, if they ever convince him, he's even more likely to think we're still alive and come looking for us, isn't he?"

"Let's prepare for the worst," his mother replied.

"Try it now!" Rufus called out an hour later. Arabella unhitched the oxen and led them a short distance from the clearing they'd found. Elizabeth pressed her hands to her face, peering anxiously over the top of her fingertips.

Henry pushed a screwdriver into a recess on the side of the folded house and gave a firm twist. There was a short pause . . . and then the house began to unfold. Like the petals of a flower at daybreak it unfurled, the walls fanning out and interlocking with one another. Clunk! Clunk!

"Incredible," Rufus breathed. He couldn't wait to tell Madeline about this!

A bush at the edge of the clearing crumpled as the

house spread to fill its allotted area. The windows fanned out and locked themselves into place with one click after another, and the roof bloomed upward and outward as a peacock's tail might, the tiles aligning themselves like soldiers on parade day. Finally, the chimneys rose up smoothly through the roof ridges to take their rightful places atop the house. And then all was still.

"Now, that's a home worth protecting," Henry said. He was clutching his cap to his chest as a sign of respect to the genius of Clement Breeze.

Rufus unhooked the centripetal rose-hub from his toolbelt and held it up.

"I'm going to try to get the defenses working," he announced. Then as he looked down at it, he remembered something. He stepped toward Henry to whisper. "When I went to see your cousin in the scrap quarter, he'd been tied up, I—"

"He's fine," Henry interrupted. "It wasn't him they were after . . ." He pointed at the centripetal rose-hub. "Treat it well and it should do wonders for you."

Rufus grinned and ran inside. He felt like whooping with delight to be back. Inside, it was a bit of a mess, but nothing seemed broken. Already he found he could not remember where the folds in the walls had been because the hinges and mechanisms were so well hidden. Quickly, he headed upstairs to tidy himself up before he began work.

"We'd better be going," Arabella said to Elizabeth outside. "We'll bring the rest of your furniture tomorrow."

"Thanks for everything," Elizabeth said. "If only everyone were more like you, perhaps . . . perhaps things would be different."

She was shivering again.

"Are you all right, Elizabeth?" Arabella asked. She pulled her scarf from her neck and wrapped it around Elizabeth. "I think you need this more than I do." Elizabeth smiled gratefully.

"I wish you luck," Henry said. "Though anyone who can escape from Tullock's lair shouldn't need it, least of all a Breeze, eh?"

Elizabeth glanced around the wood that tightly embraced the house. It was late now and eerily quiet. It always amazed her how so much snow could fall without making a noise. She wrapped her arms around herself and went inside. It was good to be home.

## THIRTY-ONE

# A Place of Splendor

It had been another long weary trudge across the desert. But finally the high and noble walls of Tresedira were starting to gain definition through the shimmering heat haze of the afternoon.

"Almost there!" Sebastian shouted over the clicking and whirring of his perambulator fan. "Tresedira! Your saviors are coming!"

Mesmer gave an enthusiastic yap.

But Madeline wasn't paying any attention to Sebastian's posturing. She was trailing behind and watching the waist-high dust devils that were spinning and swirling a little way off.

"Distant cousins of the shoofas?" she mused as she tugged on her father's arm and pointed them out. They watched as one of the miniature cyclones engulfed a dead bush, lacerated it into tiny pieces and then blew itself out, disappearing into thin air with a faint whistle.

"There's certainly a lot of blowy energy knocking

around in weird guises," she went on. "I wonder if it's related to the strange weather all around Pinrut. It makes you think . . ."

"It's almost like the aftershock of some major elemental event," her father agreed.

Suddenly the nearest dust devil swooped toward Philip and he disappeared into a cyclone of sand that flipped him onto his back.

"Argh!" he howled. "Get off!"

"Father!" Madeline cried.

"Stay back!" Philip yelled just as the vicious miniature hurricane burned itself out and joined the desert wind with its own mournful whistle.

"I suggest we move a little faster," Philip said, getting to his feet and dusting himself down with shaky hands. Another dust devil sprang up to their right.

"In fact, let's get inside the town walls now," Philip added.

He grabbed Madeline's hand and they started to run, the blades on their perambulator fans whirring noisily as their legs pounded the desert sand.

"Come on, Mr. Silver, Mesmer!" Madeline called as they strode past, and her father dropped her hand to urge Turnip and the fans onward.

"That's what I like to see," Sebastian exclaimed. "Enthusiasm! Yes, pick up the pace, Turnip. Time to deliver your magnificent goods!"

Tresedira was a place of splendor. Toward the center of town colorful towers pointed at the deep blue sky like elegant fingers. And on the roads leading inward to this central hub, many of the buildings were made of a pale marble with golden veins running through it. The roofs boasted elaborate terra-cotta tiles, and sinuous vines with luscious-looking purple grapes snaked their way up mosaic-covered walls and across decorative wrought-iron balconies.

Tiny monkeys sat on window ledges chewing on the grapes and spitting the pips at passersby.

"It's strange to see a town without snow," Madeline said, her eyes darting around with wonder. "And hard to believe a place can be so *beautiful*."

Sebastian, however, was interested only in the inhabitants of Tresedira. Although most people wore light cotton clothes—tunics and dresses—they looked extremely hot. They languished on balconies, swaying lazily in hammocks, or sat in shaded doorways, perspiration glistening on their brows. And those that were going about their work looked even hotter.

"This is the pot of gold at the end of the rainbow," Sebastian whispered fiercely. "When these people see what we have in this cart . . ." He could barely contain his excitement. Madeline's father wasn't much calmer.

The chattering perambulator fans the group wore were already starting to cause a commotion by the time they reached the town square. The townsfolk were pointing at the contraptions and muttering to one another.

Sebastian crossed to the fountain at the center of the square. Madeline followed, ducking under a giant banner as she did so:

**TRESEDIRA COMPETITION WEEK**
**IT'S HOT, HOT, HOT!**

Now she noticed in the odd doorway and window the occasional person deep in concentration as they labored over something carefully hidden from view.

"Hmm. Some kind of competition in progress, I would say," Sebastian mused.

"What remarkable powers of observation you possess, Mr. Silver," Madeline said drily. "I mean, how could you *possibly* know?"

Studiously ignoring Madeline's last remark, Sebastian spread his arms wide with excitement. "But we have no interest in competitions anyway. Let's set up shop. These people will love you, Mr. Breeze. Look at them! They're all sweating like pigs!"

A haughty-looking woman with hoop earrings and chubby arms turned to Sebastian in passing. "I *beg* your pardon, sir," she snapped.

"Not you, madam. You glisten like the morning dew."

Sebastian gave the woman his most charming smile. She broke into an unexpected girlish giggle, batted her eyelashes and scurried away.

Madeline and her father set out the fans for sale. They activated a dozen, pointing their whirring blades and flapping paddles skyward, and Madeline threw some red cactus flower petals over them, to demonstrate the powerful air currents they created. She tied her favorite butterfly back to the corner of the cart, and its colored glass wings caught the sun as they flapped, throwing multicolored patches of light onto the square. People soon started to draw close, leaving the shade, their eyes wide with fascination and longing.

"Seems you two have a fan club," Sebastian said. Then he cupped his hands around his mouth and bellowed, "Form an orderly line, people! Let's hear your spondoolies jangling!"

Madeline had to admit, Mr. Silver knew how to get his customers' attention. She gave her father a relieved smile. Then, just as Madeline was plucking her beloved monkey fan from the cart, things started to go wrong—again. She noticed a man in a blue military uniform marching toward them across the square. He had a thin moustache, narrowed eyes and a pompous air about him. Strands of lank dark hair poked out from under a peaked cap covered in gold braid. Rather bizarrely, considering the heat, his silver buttons looked like snowflakes. And Madeline thought there was something vaguely familiar about him.

He ripped an ax from a chopping block as he approached Madeline's father. The ax owner raised his hand to complain but then, seeing who it was, thought better of it.

The military man stopped a short distance away from Philip, clicked his heels together and waved the ax at the cart.

"I'm Captain Stubbings, head of the Tresedira Guard," he said in polished tones. "And I'm impounding this little lot."

"Not again," Madeline sighed.

"On what grounds?" her father demanded. "We are here to serve the people of Tresedira with the famous Breeze family fans. We're not letting you take anything."

"Then you leave me no choice but to destroy your stock," Stubbings said. He raised the ax above his head and charged toward the stall.

## THIRTY-TWO

# Duel in the Square!

"He won't do it. Hold firm, everyone," Madeline's father urged.

But a manic look had appeared on Stubbings's face.

"Er, I think he's serious, Father," Madeline said. She pulled at his elbow.

"Then he'll have to go through me first," he declared, puffing out his chest. "You'll see, he's full of hot air."

"Father, please move!" Madeline begged. In the next instant the ax was cleaving through the air, down toward the delicate fan clutched in her father's hands. His eyes went wide. Madeline threw herself toward the guard—but she knew she'd be too late. Then, as the ax came within an inch of removing her father's thumb, a thin sword blade whipped beneath it and halted its downward sweep. Sebastian, the wielder of the sword, gave a triumphant cry.

"All right, he's not bluffing," Philip gulped.

"Touché . . . ," Sebastian cried as he flicked the sword

upward and Stubbings and his ax staggered back. ". . . and olé!"

And Madeline watched with surprise as Sebastian revealed himself to be a master swordsman. Stubbings regained his balance and raised the ax again. Sebastian parried neatly and danced away unharmed.

"Out of the way, dandy," Stubbings grunted. "I have business with the fanmaker."

Sebastian removed his hat and threw it onto Mesmer's head with a flourish. The dog peeked out from under the brim with a worried look.

"Then you have business with me!" Sebastian replied, swishing his blade through the air with a theatrical chopping motion. The crowd "oohed" in unison and Sebastian raised a falsely modest hand to acknowledge his audience.

Then Stubbings and Sebastian began to circle each other like angry scorpions, moving across the square as they did so. The crowd followed, captivated.

Madeline surprised herself by calling out, "Be careful, Mr. Silver!" as if she really cared.

"Extraordinary lives are not lived by being careful, Madeline!" Sebastian replied.

"Wow! He never stops, does he?" Madeline remarked to Mesmer.

Suddenly Stubbings broke from his circling and swung the ax at Sebastian's head. But Sebastian was ready for him. His blade flashed and he sliced through the ax's wooden handle. The ax head thudded to the ground, throwing up a little cloud of dust.

"Ha! Now you have no ax to grind!" Sebastian crowed.

Stubbings, flushed with rage, stared at the ax handle left in his hand. Then he made a lunge for Sebastian, swinging the handle like a club. Sebastian was caught off guard, the end of the handle hit him in the chest and he staggered back. Mesmer barked sharply and bounded forward to sink his teeth into Stubbings's ankle, but with a leer the man kicked the dog back into the crowd. As Mesmer scrabbled to his feet, snarling, Madeline put a restraining hand on the dog's neck.

"Stay here, Mesmer," she pleaded. "It's safer."

"Oh, leave the man alone, Stubbings, you bully," the woman with the hoop earrings called out.

"Your support is most welcome, madam," Sebastian crooned. Regaining breath and poise he backed toward a bush of pink and red flowers and whipped off one of the flower heads with a swish of his blade. The bud flew through the air and the woman caught it, and fluttered her eyelashes in Sebastian's direction.

"I hope he doesn't kill you," she said with tenderness.

"Ah, madam, we have so much in common," Sebastian replied.

Mesmer's warning yelp came too late as Stubbings

took advantage of this romantic interlude to swipe at Sebastian's sword with his ax handle. Clang!—the blade flew from Sebastian's hand, spun through the air and stuck in a plant pot on a balcony high above. Sebastian was left holding just the hilt.

"Look at that, Mesmer," he gulped. "Never buy a sword from a man with rusty cuff links." Mesmer whined with despair.

Sebastian started to edge away from the gloating Stubbings.

"Would it be worth appealing to your sense of fair play?" he tried.

"Only if I had one," Stubbings said as he raised the ax handle for a final crushing blow.

"Mr. Silver!" Madeline plucked a large file from her toolbelt and threw it to Sebastian.

He caught it and held it above his head just in time to block the blow.

But then Stubbings's attention seemed to be caught by something on the other side of the square. Suddenly he smirked and dropped his weapon. "Let's leave it there, shall we, before somebody gets hurt." He grasped Sebastian's hand and pumped it vigorously. "Welcome to Tresedira!"

And with that he turned on his heel and headed back to his fort, which sat, squat and sandy, behind two houses in the corner of the square. Madeline did a double take as she spotted a raven perched on its ramparts. Sweltering and out of breath, Sebastian handed the file back to Madeline. It was bent at right angles.

"Now you can do corners with it," he said.

Madeline rolled her eyes, clipped the damaged tool back onto her belt and gave Sebastian his hat.

"That was all very odd, wasn't it?" she wondered out loud, gnawing nervously on the now quite stubby nail of her little finger. "Why did he just walk away like that?"

"Intimidated by my superior dueling skills," Sebastian preened.

"You're certainly full of surprises," Madeline's father observed.

"Yes, and full of yourself, Mr. Silver," Madeline added, giving him a long look. "But you risked your life to save my father, so . . . thank you."

Sebastian seemed flustered. He wasn't used to genuine gratitude, and it felt strangely . . . good. But he didn't know what to say in return. "Just protecting my investment," he blustered. Then Mesmer barked. "Yes, I know. Thrust, thrust, *then* parry." Sebastian glanced back at Madeline, his normal jokey self once more. "Everyone's a critic."

The crowd surrounded the travelers like seagulls around a fishing boat as they headed back toward the cart. The sun beat down.

"I want that pretty table fan with the beautiful colored glass pieces," said one woman, flapping at her flushed face with her hand.

"I'd like to buy two!" cried an old man. "One for each armpit!"

"There'll be enough for everyone, I'm sure," Philip said proudly.

Madeline found herself sharing a delighted grin with Sebastian. This was going to be their day after all.

Except when they got back to where they had left the cart, it wasn't there. All of the fans were gone too—apart from the monkey one, which lay upside down and half hidden in the dirt. Madeline picked it up and held it close.

The disappointed crowd dispersed rapidly back to their coveted patches of shade.

"Hey!" Sebastian called after them. "We can still take your money now. Give you the goods later." But he was talking to the backs of heads. "Ah, tortuous transactions! Even in this sweltering heat our assets are frozen!"

Madeline had a tight feeling in her throat. No wonder Stubbings had let them go so easily. As her father sank to the ground in despair, she felt all hope drain away.

## THIRTY-THREE

# Madeleine Has Another Idea

The stars shone down on Tresedira and its uncomfortably hot inhabitants. Narrow, sun-baked streets retained the heat of the day and the clicking of cicadas filled the air with a high-pitched drone.

The wooden sign for the Sleepy Scorpion inn swung creakily to and fro in the sweet-smelling warm drafts of the night air. The outside of the building was ornate, with amber stonework and closed red wooden shutters, but inside sweaty, salmon-colored walls glowed in the candlelight and flushed faces swigged from tankards. Heated arguments—literally—dipped and rose in irritable waves, but the serenely solid innkeeper just tugged at his neat little goatee, cleaned another glass and watched out for any disagreements that might turn unpleasant.

". . . years without rain," someone complained. "It's freaky, I tell you."

"Who'd have thought we'd miss it."

On the wall behind the landlord a large, pinkish chameleon, visible only by its purple shadow, swiveled its eyes about, looking for bugs.

Crushed around a corner table were Madeline, her father and Sebastian. Madeline chewed anxiously on a nail as she watched her father. He hadn't said a word since they'd found all his fans gone.

Mesmer was squeezed under the table, lapping from a bowl marked LEMONADE.

Sebastian leaned toward Madeline. "It's just water with a twist of lemon, really," he whispered, pointing down at the blue-haired dog. "He thinks he likes lemonade, but he tried it once and had hiccups for a week." Sebastian leaned back in his chair. "How's your lemonade, Mesmer?"

The dog wagged his tail enthusiastically and Sebastian laughed.

"I don't know why you're so happy, Mr. Silver." Madeline frowned. "Without the fans, you won't see any money either."

"True—it's a shame. I was sure *this* plan was going to work . . . but never mind. I'll be on my way shortly, find another way." Sebastian settled back into his seat and took a swig of ale. "Every day holds a multitude of new possibilities."

"Well, as long as *you're* all right," Madeline snapped, her amber eyes burning hot. "Don't worry about us."

Honestly, just when she was beginning to think he wasn't all bad . . . Sebastian shifted uncomfortably. The girl had a habit of making him do that—and he wasn't sure he liked it.

"I spent my entire life making those fans," Philip whispered suddenly. "So beautiful, so useful . . . it's like losing old friends."

"Perhaps we'll find them, Father," Madeline tried.

Sebastian felt a rare twinge of guilt." Yes, yes, we'll start looking tomorrow," he blustered. "Can't be far, can they?"

But Madeline had concerns that she didn't want to share in front of her father. Stubbings, so strangely familiar and who obviously did not want them here, that raven again—it was all very unsettling. Deep down, if she was honest with herself, she didn't hold out much hope for the fans. But how could she admit that to her father? Were they stuck here now, with no means or money to get back? Would she never see Rufus and her mother again?

Would Rufus have found a way to make this trip work—should she have let him come instead? She felt deflated and small.

Just then, the innkeeper waddled over and leaned across their table, his rotund belly settling like dough on the tabletop.

"Please excuse me, nice people," he said as he reached

over to the competition poster on the wall. JUST 4 SIZZLING DAYS TO GO, it read. He ripped off a small square of paper and the 4 became a 3.

"What's the competition?" Madeline asked suddenly. The red-cheeked landlord staggered back and clamped a splayed hand to his broad chest in shock as though he had just been asked what color the sky was.

"*What's the competition?* Really? Where have you been, young lady? Stuck in a snowdrift?"

"Well, yes."

"It's the famous annual inventing competition," the innkeeper went on, running the back of his hand across his moist brow. "It takes our minds off this unending heat."

"What are the rules?"

"Simply this: the contestant must startle, amaze and inspire!" he roared.

"And anyone can enter?" Madeline asked, an idea forming.

"Of course! Even my cat entered last year," he said with a mischievous twinkle. "Came to nothing—didn't put the hours in." The landlord spread his arms wide and motioned around the crowded inn. "Some of the folk around here have been working on their little contraptions and gizmos all year. First prize is huge—one hundred gold coins!"

That would more than pay back our loan, Madeline

calculated. And leave money over for making new fans . . .

Suddenly a brawl erupted at the bar and the innkeeper hurried away. "Hey, I'll have none of that fur flying in my establishment. Take it outside, boys, or make like gentlemen and buy each other a relaxing Sleepy Scorpion special. I put the little umbrellas in for you, no?"

"Enter the competition, Father," Madeline said, her voice breathless. "Make the best fan you've *ever* made—it's bound to win, especially here!"

Philip jolted to earth and looked at his daughter. His brilliant daughter. A light started to dance in the golden flecks of his eyes.

"But I'll need a workshop," he began to mumble to himself. "And some good materials, oh, and paper to draw up plans and—"

"But there's only three days to go," Sebastian said.

"I think I can do it," Philip countered.

"Of course you can, Father."

He flexed his fingers. "Wouldn't it be fantastic to go home with a hundred gold coins!" he said.

Across the square in the Tresedira fort, Captain Stubbings was bathed in sweat and hacking away dangerously at a piece of wood with a rusty saw. He glanced sideways at the calendar pinned to the crumbling plasterwork by his head.

"Only three more days," he grunted to himself, sawing even faster.

Just then a prim-looking soldier stepped into the room. His blond hair was flattened to perfection, and carefully applied wax shaped an elaborate quiff off to one side. He clicked his heels together and Stubbings looked up.

"What is it, Sergeant Catgut?" Stubbings snapped.

"I had someone destroy the fans, Captain." Catgut brushed a splinter fussily from his jacket as he spoke.

Stubbings ran a hairy forearm across his brow and spat a mouthful of dusty phlegm on the floor. "Good," he said. "You can send that gruesome bird back then. We've carried out our orders."

Stubbings returned to his frantic sawing, and with a sharp twang! the saw blade snapped in half and the piece of wood he was leaning on flew up and hit him in the head. Catgut winced.

"Argh!" Stubbings yelled, staggering backward.

"Captain, forgive me if I speak out of turn," Catgut said. "But are you not in danger of forgetting your position?"

"Since when does being head of the guard mean you can't be creative? Hmm?" Stubbings said. "I want people to see another side of me." His eyes glazed over in wistful reverie. "I want people to say, Yes, he'll lock you in a locust-infested dungeon if you steal an apple but, boy, will he do it with flair: the chains arranged just so, window bars polished, locusts scattered around tasteful like, not all clumped in a corner."

"That's beautiful, Captain," Catgut said. "But I am still concerned about Breeze. Apparently he is entering the competition. Someone overheard him talking in the Sleepy Scorpion."

Stubbings rubbed at his throbbing head. "Blistering armpits! That's all I need, a flaming professional craftsman to compete against!"

"May I suggest a shift of focus, Captain?" Catgut said. "I don't think your cousin would like this turn of events either. Are you forgetting that when the weather turned inexplicably hot and dry all those years ago, he provided you with the funds to step up and practically run this town? All you had to do in return was keep people from straying toward Pinrut, talking about sunshine. He made you everything you are, Captain. And goodness knows I have worked insanely hard to gain his trust too—"

"Huh! *Groveled* hard, more like," Stubbings interrupted with a snort.

Catgut sucked in air through his teeth and did his best to ignore this slur. "I'm just saying we want to retain his trust, and he will be *far* from happy if . . ."

Stubbings sighed suddenly and threw the remains of his saw down in a sulk. "Fine!" he snapped. "We'll just have to find some way of nobbling this idiot Breeze, won't we?"

"I'll send a message, make sure your cousin is fully informed." Catgut pushed back his sleeves, tucked his chin into his neck and moved toward the raven with a deeply distasteful expression.

# THIRTY-FOUR

# Scratskin's Luck

Rufus, hair parted neatly once more, was kneeling in the kitchen with the house defense plans that he'd been working on all day. He raised his mallet and, with a hefty strike, smashed a hole in the paneled wall in front of him. With the connection to the underground workshop severed, he had to find some other point to attach the centripetal rose-hub.

Rods, ratchets and cogs stared back at him from the shattered woodwork. Yes, as the plans suggested, this could be a place to embed it. All the metal rods would have to be cut and then rearranged to funnel directly into the rose-hub, though. Complicated. For a moment Rufus wondered if he could do it, but then he heard Madeline's brave voice in his head: "You'd be much better at figuring that out than me." He smiled, grabbed a small saw and began to work.

In the sitting room his mother, wrapped tightly in a blanket, was staring out the window at the wood beyond.

She felt so cold. It was as though ice were running through her veins. Only her husband's arms around her once more would banish this insidious frost that had invaded her body.

But maybe Philip and Madeline were already safely on their way back with pockets full of gold, she told herself.

She looked out at snow piling up on a thousand branches, two snowy owls perched side by side, blinking slowly, their heads turning to and fro.

She hoped it remained this peaceful. She hoped she wouldn't see the glint of armor anytime soon.

Scratskin's lidless eyes flicked from tree to tree, taking in the scraped bark, a broken branch here and there. He licked his swollen gums and looked down at the map in his bony hands. Was it really possible the Great Snow Bear had strayed from its usual territory in Reffinock forest and wandered north into Thorn Wood? For surely only something as big as the bear could leave such a destructive trail.

It was getting dark but Scratskin strode onward stealthily, searching for further clues. Then something unexpected suddenly caught his gaze, nestled in among the trees. Not the muscular, fur-covered creature he was seeking but something else. Scratskin allowed himself a congratulatory sneer at his fortuitous discovery. Then he headed back to share it with his master.

The next morning, at the top of Scratskin's tower, Tullock tapped on the greasy wood of his servant's door with a shudder.

"Enter if you must—again."

As his eyes grew accustomed to the gloom, Tullock could just make out Scratskin hunched over a desk.

"Why did you call for me, Scratskin?" Tullock snapped. "And shouldn't I be the one summoning you?" he added under his breath.

Scratskin held up a bony finger. "One moment. I am finishing off a nameplate for the Great Snow Bear," he replied. He dragged a long sharpened fingernail across a brass plate, etching another letter into the metal. Tullock winced at the noise. "I may not have the mighty beast yet. But my chance will come . . ." Scratskin made another scratch in the metal, setting Tullock's teeth on edge this time.

"Do that later, Scratskin, please! Now why am I here?!"

With a petulant huff, Scratskin left his chair and moped to where the hole in the wall he had punched for his raven still allowed flurries of snow to waft in intermittently and gather in small, slushy piles. From his pocket he pulled a rather blackened-looking pipe, lit it with a match and was almost instantly enveloped in a sickly, green fug, which he puffed out in the direction of the wall opening.

Scratskin's large lidless eyes stared at Tullock through the putrid mist for what seemed like a very long time. "I found something *unusual* in the woods last night," Scratskin announced finally.

A shudder passed down Tullock's spine. His eyes darted anxiously around the room.

"Is it, er, here—now, lurking under something?"

Scratskin paused for a moment, enjoying his master's squirming.

"No. It wasn't an animal," he admitted eventually. "I found the Breeze house. And there was smoke coming from the chimney."

"Really," Tullock smirked. But his swagger was short-lived, for in the next moment, Scratskin's raven swept in through the hole in the wall with a raucous shriek. Tullock staggered back, his hand clutching at his hammering heart. It was horror upon horrors in Scratskin's world.

Scratskin pulled a message from the raven's leg and handed it to Tullock, who scanned the scrawly writing and scowled.

"Get down to the Breeze house. Order the Hammer Squad to destroy it," Tullock barked. "And knowing them, go prepared for anything."

"And what of the woman and the boy?"

Tullock hesitated for a moment. Elizabeth's lovely face hovered before him. He looked down at the message again. This was no time for faltering.

"Don't care. Lose them in a snowdrift somewhere," Tullock instructed. He flicked at the message. "And while you do that, I must turn my attention to this irritating little matter."

## THIRTY-FIVE

# A Grisly End

The centripetal rose-hub was in place. Twenty-three fine copper tubes ran away from it like rays from a sun, each leading to its own special part in the house defenses. Rufus was fumbling with a final tube but could not get it to reach.

He glanced over his shoulder through the door at his mother, who was still bundled in blankets and hunched next to the sitting-room stove. She'd been dozing there all night while he worked. She seemed smaller somehow, and he was alarmed at her pallor. Her usually light green eyes seemed dark now in contrast to the whiteness of her skin. Even her flame-red hair had turned dull. Her tired eyes flicked to meet his.

"Sorry. I'm not being much help, Ru. I'm feeling a bit lazy at the moment."

"You're allowed to be lazy when you have a cold," Rufus replied with a cheeriness he didn't feel.

Is that what they were calling it? A cold? She clutched the blankets more tightly around her aching body.

"Tell me about Pinrut before the snow came?" Rufus asked as he turned back to his work. He and Madeline had asked this many times before, but they never grew tired of hearing the answer. And right now he wanted the comfort of hearing his mother talk. Her quiet slide into this colorless stupor was frightening him—and he couldn't think of a plan to stop it.

"Sunny," Elizabeth replied. She coughed weakly, then continued. "There were flowers everywhere and there was fruit on the trees. We used to go on picnics, have school lessons outside, camp under the stars." Elizabeth stared into the flickering flames.

"I'm proud you and Father stood up to the Tullocks all these years," Rufus said as he fought to bend the tube in his hand. "Because—"

"There's movement, Rufus," his mother interrupted. "A disturbance in the wood."

Sure enough, branches were bobbing in the distance, shedding their loads of snow.

Rufus turned back to the mechanism, his heart starting to pound. What he was doing wasn't working. What would Madeline do? She'd approach the problem creatively.

Suddenly he had an idea. It was from no textbook and amounted to chaos compared with his usual orderly way of working, but it might just do the job. He grabbed the kitchen-stove poker, rapidly sawed a short length off the end and fired up his blowtorch.

They were coming. Elizabeth could see distant shapes now—armor in the spaces between the white limbs of the trees, like silver shavings in flour.

"How are you doing, Rufus?" she asked calmly. But he could hear the fear hidden beneath her voice. His hands shook as he turned the tube over, making sure the welded add-on was true all the way around.

Helmets now. Visible. Hammers in hands, ready for action. And the sinister form of Scratskin leading them. Elizabeth shuddered.

"They're here," she said as Rufus fitted the final tube.

"I shall count to three!" Scratskin's words came slithering through the windows and walls. "Then the hammering begins. Please, there's no need to come out. You'll have a much better view from inside."

"Have mercy!" Elizabeth called out.

"Tullock asked me to tell you the time for mercy has passed—your debt will never be fully repaid!" Scratskin called back. "And though his orders rarely interest me, I shall carry out this one with relish! Hammer Squad, on your mark, one . . ."

All twenty-four tubes were connected. Fingers crossed, Rufus shoved what was left of the fire poker into the rose-hub's center to use as a lever, and yanked.

". . . two . . . ," Scratskin cried.

The Hammer guards raised their heavy hammers high as one.

Inside the house a sequential shudder rippled through its walls. From all directions, Rufus could hear joints and pivots shunting and groaning.

". . . three . . ."

Bam, bam, bam!

For a moment Rufus thought it was the sound of hammers hitting their home—but no. Instead, he saw thick metal shutters folding out over all the windows and doors, slamming into place. He heard the metal grilles in the chimneys fan into position too.

"Yes!" Rufus crowed. "We have lockdown!"

His mother smiled at him with relief. It was dark inside the house now, but it felt safe, like being hidden in a cave while a storm brewed outside.

Moments later the storm began. The clanging of the Hammer Squad hammers resounded through the house. Rufus and his mother clapped their hands to their ears. It was like being inside an enormous bell. *Baroom, baroom, baroom!* But the metal panels remained impenetrable. Eventually the noise stopped and Scratskin's voice just filtered through to Elizabeth and Rufus.

"Tricky! *Very* tricky. But I'm afraid this house *will* fall!"

A strange scratching sound followed.

Rufus bounded over to a window. He peered through

a slit in the metal plating that covered it and bit his lip. Right at the very edge of his vision he could just make out Scratskin working away at the metal plating with the biggest, most fearsome-looking metal cutters he had ever seen.

"Scratskin's still trying to get in," Rufus said. He twirled his cuff links nervously. He trusted his grandfather's defenses, but it was chilling hearing Tullock's manservant scratching at their home like this.

Then Scratskin turned suddenly, scuttled over and jammed his ghastly face up against the window plating. He stared directly into Rufus's eyes.

"I *will* get in," he sneered loudly. "And then my cutters will do the talking."

Rufus jumped back. He thought his heart was going to burst! He took a deep breath to calm himself. What more could he do to keep his mother safe?

"Go away, you bag of knuckles," Elizabeth spluttered from across the room.

But Scratskin's reply was drowned out by a sudden, ground-shaking roar. All the cutlery in the dresser rattled, and ornaments danced along shelves.

"I recognize that roar," Elizabeth said in amazement.

Outside the window, Rufus saw Scratskin's expression change. "The Great Snow Bear," he mouthed, disbelief mingling with obvious desire.

The members of the Hammer Squad were shuffling anxiously—terrified by something Rufus could not yet see.

But Scratskin was standing his ground, his bulging eyes alight. "Don't just stand there, fools!" he shrieked at the Hammer Squad. "Fetch my trapping gear from the carriage! I'll keep the beast busy! Hurry!"

The guards retreated hastily into the forest.

"At last we meet," Scratskin gushed.

Rufus watched as the creature finally shambled into view. He sucked in his breath. It was colossal. So majestic and white.

"Impressive, isn't it?" his mother said quietly from behind him.

"It's enormous," Rufus said. "I think Scratskin intends to kill it, but I don't see how he can . . ."

"You stay here with me, my beauty," Rufus and his mother could just hear Scratskin cooing. "My men will be back soon with a wonderful apparatus I'd be honored to show you."

Elizabeth said nothing, but she allowed herself the tiniest of smiles. Sometimes when things were at their most bleak, it seemed justice stepped forward to take a bow.

"Hurry, you fools!" Scratskin screamed into the woods. "Bring my traps!" His words echoed back to him emptily.

But at the sudden loud noise the Great Snow Bear reared up on its hind legs. It loomed over Scratskin, a towering edifice of quivering fur and muscle. Rufus had to squat down and peer up through the hole to see the beast's head.

"That's it!" Scratskin said. His eyes were glowing now, his pupils big and black like frogspawn. "That's how I shall immortalize you. Hold that pose!"

But the bear did not hold its pose. With an indignant swipe at the metal cutters that Scratskin held protectively before himself, the bear batted them to the ground and snapped them in two with a heavy paw.

"But—" Scratskin rasped.

It was the last word he spoke.

The bear reared again, bared its mighty fangs and fell forward like an avalanche. With a bellow that rippled throughout the forest it crushed Scratskin flat. The odious man lay pressed into the snow, broken, lifeless, his look of horror frozen.

Rufus staggered back and turned away from the window, clamping his fist to his mouth. He couldn't watch. Where were the Hammer Squad—why hadn't they come back to help? He remembered how Scratskin had attacked one of their members on Tullock's behalf just yesterday. Perhaps they had never intended to return.

Minutes passed and a snowy silence descended once more.

"If that was the best Tullock could do, I don't see anyone breaking in now," Rufus whispered finally. "We've nothing else to fear, Mother. We just wait for Madeline and Father to return."

But his mother said nothing. Rufus raised his head sharply to look at her. She was bent forward, shaking uncontrollably. He rushed to her side as she turned her face up to him. There were bumps now covering her pale skin. They were most peculiar. They were shaped like snowflakes.

"Oh, no," Rufus gasped.

"Pinrutian flu," his mother said, her voice as thin as rice paper. "I knew it was. I'm so sorry, Ru."

"You've nothing to be sorry for," Rufus said. "What can I do? How can I help?"

"You can't do anything," she replied. "You must look out for yourself now."

## THIRTY-SIX

# Impossibly Intricate Designs

Madeline took one last anxious look around—the narrow backstreet was deserted—then closed the door and clattered down the steps to join her father, Sebastian and Mesmer. She had insisted vehemently that they keep the workshop a secret, though Sebastian had laughed and her father had barely noticed her words. The competition was the answer to all their problems, but for precisely that reason she had a niggling feeling someone would want to stop them. And she couldn't help wondering if that someone had something to do with Tullock, even at this distance. She just couldn't shake the feeling, however silly it was.

The workshop had smooth sandstone walls and a colorful, intricate mosaic floor, which occasional tiny red salamanders scuttled across. It was well stocked, with shelves full of hand tools almost as good as the Breezes' own, boxes of scrap metal, two sturdy workbenches and a large freestanding lathe. All of which were covered in layers of dust and spiders' webs. The place was almost entirely underground so it had no windows in the walls, but circular skylights overhead threw cylindrical shafts of dust-filled early morning sunlight downward, like glowing pillars. Madeline's father sat on a stool in the middle of the room. Motionless. He was staring into space, his features transfixed in a kind of stupefied bliss.

"Is he all right?" Sebastian whispered.

"He's working," Madeline replied.

"He is?"

But Sebastian couldn't see what the fanmaker could.

All around Madeline's father, floating in space, cogs whirred and interconnected, switches clicked to and fro, pistons pumped, pushrods shunted back and forth, calculations jostled and cool air currents wafted.

Suddenly Philip snapped to and frowned. His left eyebrow arched quizzically. He threw a thin strip of metal onto a nearby stool and pushed it with his foot into one of the shafts of sunlight.

"So you like the workshop then, Father?" Madeline asked.

"Hmm?" he replied dreamily. "Oh, yes, amazing how you found one so quickly."

The piece of metal on the stool was beginning to bend slightly in the sun's heat. A smile tugged at the corners of Philip's mouth.

"It was a humiliating experience," Sebastian shuddered. "Blooma Bantree—the lady with the hoop earrings, the one so impressed with my dueling skills—as luck would have it, her late uncle was a clockmaker. All she wanted in payment was to hug the mysterious swordsman!" Sebastian winced. "And my ribs will never be the same." Mesmer let out a sympathetic whimper.

But Madeline's father wasn't listening. He was examining the bending metal with a set of magnifying goggles.

"And for risking life and limb in Blooma's embrace do I still get twenty percent of the winnings, Mr. Breeze?" Sebastian added.

Philip was sketching now and didn't reply.

"Yes, Mr. Silver," Madeline answered for him. "I didn't doubt for a moment that you'd want your slice of the prize money."

Madeline watched her father as he fell deeper and deeper into his own unreachable world. She longed to go with him, to help him shape his latest vision, but she knew she had to be the sensible one and keep an eye open for any more trouble.

"I'm going to try one last time to find out what happened to Turnip and the fans, then I'll keep watch outside—just in case," she said as she filled a jug with water from a pump in the corner of the workshop and placed it down next to her father alongside a chipped cup. But he didn't answer. Madeline suddenly felt very lonely.

Then Sebastian spoke. "Superlative idea!" he exclaimed. He gave her a warm smile, which Madeline found herself returning gratefully.

She headed for the staircase, the one surviving precious monkey fan hooked to her toolbelt for comfort.

"Don't forget to drink. It's hot down here," Madeline added as she turned away from her father sadly. "Come on, Mesmer!" The dog sprang up the wooden steps beside her.

Madeline, Sebastian and Mesmer spent a few hours in Tresedira's endless dark alleyways, peering into the shadows, hoping to catch a glimpse of a cartwheel, the glint of a fan blade or the swish of Turnip's tail. But Madeline knew in her heart the fans were gone, so they finally took up a watchful position sitting on the stone step outside her father's workshop door.

The streets remained empty, however, as people "invented"— perhaps she was worrying needlessly. Madeline cracked the tail on the monkey fan and watched as it sprang off the workshop door and hovered above them, ears flapping, eyes twinkling, its spinning tail washing a welcome cool draft in their direction. Some curious Tresedira monkeys hopped closer to investigate.

Mesmer flopped affectionately onto Madeline's feet, and she was pleasantly surprised to find herself enjoying Mr. Silver's presence as they sat in companionable silence—he was a lot more bearable when he wasn't showing off or trying to sell something. As they were sitting there, a man with a beard like a tumbleweed walked past, leading a weather-beaten old horse.

It was Turnip.

Madeline and Sebastian nearly fell over each other in their rush to intercept them.

The horse nuzzled its nose against Madeline and whinnied. Mesmer gave a short, cheerful bark in reply.

"Get away! This is my horse!" the old man snapped.

Gray hair sprouted like moss from his ears and nostrils.

"But this noble steed is our splendid friend Turnip," Sebastian pronounced.

"*I* found him running wild. He's *mine*," the man snorted. "Unless—you got any gold?"

"Er, no," Sebastian admitted. "You catch me between funds, unfortunately."

"I'll give you this for him." Her face pale, Madeline held out the monkey-shaped fan.

The man grimaced at the offering. "Well, what is it?"

Madeline cracked the tail again and the monkey leaped into action once more. As it flipped off Turnip's side and into the air, the old man watched in awe. When the tail-driven breeze reached his face, his eyes closed in bliss.

"Truly takes the heat off," the man mumbled, almost smiling now. "Done! Have him." He thrust a tatty piece of rope into Madeline's hand and walked away, guiding his new fan overhead with a stick.

Madeline wiped her eyes quickly, tied Turnip to the wall and resumed her vigil on the workshop step.

Sebastian was shocked. "That fan was the last of the Breeze legacy."

"But in the end it is just a thing," Madeline said thoughtfully after a long silence. "Whatever Father says, fantastic and wonderful as the Breeze fans are, or were, they remain just objects all the same. But Turnip—he is flesh and blood, and a friend." Madeline patted the horse as he drank deeply from a trough. She glanced at Sebastian, who suddenly seemed lost in thought. "You don't have to wait here with me, Mr. Silver. Why don't you go to the Sleeping Scorpion for a while if you prefer?"

Sebastian sat back down on the step and Mesmer leaned up against him. "I'll stay if it's all the same to you. Blooma Bantree frequents the inn and I find her mildly terrifying."

"Well, it's good to have the company. Thank you."

Sebastian flushed, then gestured at the workshop door. The sound of sawing could just be made out. "But in the main I'm protecting my investment, of course."

She smiled. "Naturally."

As Tresedira fell into the soft orange glow of dusk, Madeline returned to the workshop to check on her father. She had never seen him so fired up. His brow glistened with sweat as he hunched over his work. A constellation of shimmering components covered every available surface, cogs intertwined with such precision it made Madeline gasp. Thin brass tubes stood upright on the workbenches like long grass, and a complex arrangement of lenses was throwing beams of light wildly around the room. Madeline wished Rufus was there with her to witness their father at the very peak of his talents. Even she couldn't begin to grasp what he was making, but she could resist no more, regardless.

"Can I help, Father?" she asked.

"Could you ascertain the focal lengths of those lenses, Sunshine?" her father mumbled distractedly.

"I'll try," Madeline replied.

"And how may I be of assistance, Maestro Breeze?" Sebastian called down from the top of the steps.

"Perhaps you could work out the thermal index of that oscillating spring box, Sebastian?" Philip replied.

Sebastian looked blank. "Yes, maybe I'll go and rustle us up some nibbles instead," he said, nudging Mesmer out the door.

## THIRTY-SEVEN

# A Guest Judge

The sun was at its blazing apex. The glare and ferocious heat would normally have sent the people of Tresedira scurrying for shade, but this was a special day—competition-judging day. The crowd gathered in the square, mopped their glistening brows and flapped their hands at their glowing cheeks, but they remained on tiptoe with interest. Dozens of inventions had already been displayed and demonstrated. Some weird and wonderful, some ugly but functional, some that didn't work at all: scorpion-powered hair trimmers, hats that scared off vultures, furniture made from sand, camel-spit wine—it had been quite a morning. And now there were only three entries left to be revealed. They were lined up side by side, each one covered in sacking.

Madeline stood with Sebastian and Mesmer in the crowd and watched her father as he swayed with exhaustion next to his entry. It was as tall as he was, and its sharp corners strained at the rough covering.

It had been a mad, feverish night of work, and Madeline too was dizzy with lack of sleep. She could barely remember if they had actually finished the machine, or whether it was whole and functional purely in her imagination. Captain Stubbings swaggered on the spot by the next covered device, occasionally glancing with venom at her father. But surely, with all these witnesses around, he couldn't sabotage them now.

Madeline shifted her attention to Felix Middling, a thin, twittery man with round spectacles and a startled look about him, who was hovering by the third covered competition entry.

On a grand podium to one side of the square the round, jolly-looking mayor of Tresedira slapped a hand down on his thick gray hair, then punched the air with excitement. Competition day was far and away his favorite day of the year. He pointed at Stubbings with a stocky finger.

"Captain Stubbings, show the good people of Tresedira how you intend to startle and amaze them!" he exclaimed.

Stubbings pressed one hand to his chest and tweaked his moustache with the other. "It's a long and difficult road being a creative soul, a composer even, and—"

"Get on with it!" cried the innkeeper, hot and irritable, whose bulk was wedged in the middle of the throng.

"Yes, we're melting here," said Blooma Bantree, perspiration dripping from her hoop earrings.

With a clumsy attempt at a flourish, Stubbings whipped off the burlap to reveal a crank handle attached by a series of chains and bellows to a collection of battered horns, whistles, flutes and mutilated stringed instruments. Madeline and Sebastian raised their eyebrows simultaneously.

Catgut, standing nearby, cringed with embarrassment. The crowd didn't make a sound.

Stubbings nodded slowly. "Your astonishment is completely understandable," he said. "Tresedira, I give you the gift of sweet, sweet music!" And he began to turn the handle feverishly. In the broiling heat it wasn't long before he was bathed in sweat and panting like a dog. Meanwhile, the noise coming from his "musical" invention was an alarming mix of low parping and high-pitched warbling.

Madeline winced and wedged her fingers in her ears. Somewhere a number of cats started wailing. Suddenly something snapped and a piece of tubing went spinning through the air.

"Duck!" Sebastian exclaimed.

A moment later there was the sound of smashing pottery.

"Argh! That vase was priceless!" called a distraught voice from inside a house that faced on to the square.

"I admit it's new and challenging to the ear!" Stubbings panted, clutching his shoulder as though he'd pulled a muscle.

The mayor, for once, was speechless. His mouth hung agape.

"Er, thank you, Captain Stubbings, for that unique glimpse into what you've been doing in your spare time," he said finally. "Next up, Tresedira's resident maestro, Felix Middling!"

Felix tucked his wild copper hair behind his ears nervously and tugged his canvas away to reveal a small round table. On it was a short metal man wearing a chef's hat and surrounded by plates of food.

"We humans love food. But so does mold! Especially in this heat!" Felix announced.

The crowd sighed in agreement.

"Fight back with Toby the Tester!" Felix responded.

He moved a plate of cheese in front of the metal man and pulled a lever in his back. The stout figure bowed forward with a squeak, and his mouth hinged open and sliced off a small sample of cheese. The crowd waited in silence while the metal man gurgled away, his little chin grinding in circles. Suddenly puffs of green steam shot from Toby's silver ears, and he spat his mouthful out onto the table with a "plugh!"

"Do NOT eat this cheese!" Felix exclaimed triumphantly. The crowd burst into applause. Madeline caught her father's eye as he clapped along. It was impressive—in a weird kind of way.

At last, the mayor waddled to the edge of his podium and called for silence.

"And now, finally, a welcome entrant from far afield, Mr. Philip Breeze!" he announced.

Madeline felt her heart begin to beat hard as all eyes turned to her father. She felt desperately worried for him. It mattered to her that he won—the money would save their family. But she knew it mattered to him even more. She felt her cheeks burn hot as he dragged the cloth from his invention.

A gasp of delight went through the crowd.

"Genius!" Mr. Silver muttered at Madeline's side.

It was a work of art, glittering and sparkling in the early afternoon sun. Hundreds of tiny oval glass panes, which, packed together in a circle, resembled the head of a sunflower, captured the sunshine and concentrated its golden light on the dozens of slender steel rods beneath. The rods were already bending slightly with the intense heat, and their movement began to power a complex gear mechanism that pushed from the center of the packed lenses an articulated arm with a star-shaped collection of wafer-thin fan blades on the end of it, finely decorated with swirling patterns and embedded with red and gold glass.

The dry, hot wind that blew around the town caressed

the bowed rods, and a faint melody drifted off them like a harp being plucked.

Suddenly the machine began to hum and whine. The blades started to spin. The articulated arm swayed to and fro like a hypnotic snake, cooling those in the immediate vicinity in all directions. The crowd shifted toward it. Madeline noticed that the gold flecks in her father's eyes were shining, and she felt her own spark of excitement and hope fluttering in her stomach. It was magnificent and it was working.

"Now, that's cool," Madeline said softly to no one in particular.

Sebastian grinned and removed his hat to let the breeze ruffle his hair.

"But how is it working?" someone from the crowd called. "You're not doing anything. There's no switch."

"It's powered by the heat of the sun," her father replied. "I had forgotten the strength it had."

"So clever," Blooma Bantree declared. She batted her eyelashes in Philip's direction, making Madeline wince and Sebastian smirk.

"You've won for sure!" the innkeeper exclaimed jauntily.

Madeline felt a surge of real hope—they *could* win this—and as she watched her father raise his fist in jubilation, she knew he felt it too.

"So there we have it!" called the mayor. "All of the

entries have been revealed! It only remains for me to introduce this year's judge."

The crowd fell silent with expectation.

"He is a late replacement, but do not fear, he is a man of immense standing and impeccable taste. A cousin of someone we all know well. He has traveled a long, long way to be with us today, so please offer a warm welcome to millionaire . . . Mr. Bartholomew Tullock!"

Tullock strode forth from a darkened doorway to bound up onto the podium. With his downward-sloping grin he raised his hands to quiet the applause that greeted him. Madeline's father paled visibly. She crumpled inside.

# THIRTY-EIGHT

# End of a Legacy

Madeline understood now why they had been left alone for so long. Her sense of dread had been well founded. They had come all this way to get away from this vile man and now here he was presiding over their future again. There was a kind of twisted, hateful symmetry to it. As Mesmer yelped and Sebastian caught her eye anxiously—recognizing the name—all she could do was shrug hopelessly.

Tullock shook hands with the mayor and passed him a thick, golden coin as he did so. Then he stepped forward.

"Well, what an honor," he said. "I traveled a long way to be here today, but when I heard about this wonderful competition and the hundred gold coins prize—such a life-changing sum—I knew I had to come."

Tullock gazed directly at Philip. Madeline struggled from the crowd to join her father, grabbing his hand.

"Breeze has won! It's a formality," the innkeeper exclaimed, and others agreed.

"Let's not be too hasty," Tullock boomed, his voice becoming more strident. "Mr. Breeze has produced an amusing and whimsical distraction, but where I come from, we have cold air in abundance. It's all in the eye of the beholder, after all."

"But it's a work of art too!" Blooma Bantree exclaimed. "People can live without breezes, but not without beauty."

"Rubbish! People don't *need* art, madam," Tullock snapped. His black eyes glittered. "Now, Toby the Tester impressed me very much with his practical approach to life. I know from experience that people work much harder when they're not dying of food poisoning." He pointed at Felix Middling. "You there, remind me of your name?"

"Not Felix Middling again!" Blooma cried out. "He wins every year."

"And for good reason!" Tullock said. "I declare Felix Middling to be the winner of the one hundred gold coins!"

"On behalf of Toby and myself, I thank you," Felix said, grabbing the lever on Toby's back and pushing him into a deep, squeaky bow.

The crowd applauded without much enthusiasm, except for Sergeant Catgut, who was clapping wildly. "Oh, *good* choice, Mr. Tullock!"

Stubbings only scowled.

Sebastian was feeling decidedly odd. He was not only sorely disappointed about the lack of winnings, but also experiencing a strange sinking sensation on behalf of Madeline and her father. Furthermore, although he knew he should pounce on Felix and start talking patents with him immediately, he couldn't quite bring himself to move. It was extremely unsettling—he couldn't afford to get soft in his game, his very survival was at stake. Suddenly he thought of something. Being careful to avoid being spotted by Madeline, he slunk away, Mesmer at his heels.

Madeline and her father stood silently side by side. It had all been for nothing, Madeline realized. Their hopes lay dashed once and for all.

Tullock pushed his way through the crowd to them.

"Is there a corner of this world where your sick and twisted shadow doesn't fall?" Madeline asked.

Tullock ignored her.

"Your house fell apart like paper, Windy," he sneered instead. "The Breeze legacy is no more. The last vestiges of the old order have been eradicated . . . including your wife and son."

Tears began to well in Madeline's eyes, stinging like sand from the desert, but she swallowed hard and blinked them away. He could be lying . . .

"With the house gone I greatly enjoyed watching the snow settle on those stylish fan-shaped floor tiles in your old workshop and pile up on your fine collection of blue-handled chisels."

Madeline felt as though the ground under her feet was crumbling away. How could he know a detail like that if he hadn't really seen it? If he wasn't telling the truth—about everything?

Suddenly she launched herself at Tullock with small angry fists, but her father held her back.

"Come on, Sunshine. Let's go." He broke the silence he'd kept since Tullock's judgment with a surprisingly strong voice.

"Feel free to return to Pinrut!" Tullock called after them. "I can always use extra hands in my fields. Or get lost in the desert and perish. I'm not fussy."

Philip looked down at his daughter. The color was high in her cheeks, just like her mother when she was upset, and her untamed hair lay plastered against the sheen of her forehead. What had she been through for him over the last few days?

Madeline turned her head long enough to see Tullock grab an ax from Stubbings and raise it high over the beautiful sunflower fan. "It doesn't matter," her father said simply. "It's just a machine after all."

Madeline blinked in shock to hear her father admit it so calmly.

"Let's fetch Turnip and hurry back to your mother and Rufus—they're what matter, and they need us."

"Are you *very* sad?" Madeline asked her father in a small voice as they hurried through the heat back to the workshop.

"No," he replied.

"Then why do you look it?"

"I don't look sad, Sunshine," he answered. "I look angry, with myself. I've been so selfish, so busy with my fans I've forgotten about the very people I was meant to be making them to help—my family . . ."

Madeline began to smile at him, but just then, up ahead, she saw Sebastian and Mesmer emerge from the workshop and make as if to dart away.

"Mr. Silver!" she called as she ran after him.

Sebastian stopped and turned around slowly, his face a picture of guilt. Even Mesmer seemed sheepish, his doleful eyes looking up mournfully through his blue fringe. Madeline noticed Sebastian's leather satchel, crammed to bursting with tools from the workshop. "Weren't you going to say good-bye?"

"I've squared it with the owner," Sebastian gabbled. "I can take what I like. I mean, your father won't need them now."

Madeline felt a wave of disappointment and betrayal wash over her. "Don't leave us," she whispered.

"Look, this has been a wild ride, but it's time I moved on to other fortunes. There's none to be made here anymore."

"Stay anyway—as a friend."

Sebastian looked at her for a moment, then turned away. "I can't do that. Come on, Mez."

The little dog looked up at Madeline with liquid eyes, then trotted after his friend, head bowed.

Just when she'd thought things couldn't get any worse . . . Madeline felt hollow. She had hoped there was more to Mr. Silver—but evidently there was not.

As her father trotted up on Turnip, she climbed up behind him and they galloped off in the opposite direction, eastward back to Pinrut.

# THIRTY-NINE

# An Extremely Dangerous Plan

In Pinrut, the snow fell thickly on the Breeze house hidden in Thorn Wood. The metal plating covering the door and windows was now coated in frost.

Elizabeth was in bed, her breathing shallow, her face as white as the linen sheets. The snowflake-shaped bumps on her skin were a pale blue now and more prominent.

Rufus sat by her bedside, wringing his hands and tapping his heels on the wooden floor. He felt so helpless. His gaze kept flicking to the window despite the fact that the plating kept him from seeing out.

"You're making plans, aren't you?" his mother said. Her voice was barely a whisper.

"I don't know what you mean," Rufus replied.

"Don't do anything foolish," she went on. "Tullock has risen to a new level of cruelty. If he sees you, he will show no mercy."

"I don't intend to be seen."

"Stay here," his mother urged. "Please."

"And watch you die?"

Elizabeth gave a feeble, hollow laugh. "I'm not dying. I'm just a little under the weather," she said. "And let's face it, there's a lot of weather out there."

Rufus leaned in closer and noticed the tiny blue crystals forming at the corners of his mother's mouth and eyes.

"I know the final stages of Pinrutian flu when I see them," Rufus said.

"People shake it off."

"Only with sunflower tonic." Rufus glanced toward the window again. He had no choice. Madeline would never sit by and let their mother die without trying something, whatever the risk. And neither would he.

"Do *not* go to the vault, Rufus. I mean it," his mother begged, reading his mind. "It's heavily guarded."

Rufus jumped up. He did a quick check of his toolbelt to make sure everything was present.

"You're forgetting we escaped from Tullock's mansion," he said, a sudden boldness in his voice. "How hard can it be to break into his sunflower vault?"

"Ru, please, no!"

"I'll be back soon," Rufus said. "Drink some of the soup I made for you."

He pelted down the stairs before he could change his mind and disengaged the house defenses.

As he strode out into the snow, his cloak close about

him, he tried not to think about his mother lying on her own in the dark while a strange disease turned her blood and bones to ice.

He hopped up onto the banister of the house veranda and reached under the eaves to pull the secret lever. A few seconds later the metal plating fanned back into place, making the house secure once more.

"Wait for me, Mother!" he called up to her window. "I'll be back in no time."

Rufus ran through the wood and on toward the spot where the Breeze house had once stood, stubbornly ignoring the chill of the snowstorm as it tried to permeate his layers of woolen clothing.

He was formulating a plan, and there was something he needed from his father's underground workshop. With all the snow falling, only a slight dip in the drifts indicated the whereabouts of the workshop now. Rufus had to dig deep to reach his father's tools.

It was the end of the working day in the turnip fields, and soon Henry and Arabella Bugle appeared above him, weary, dirty and low in spirits.

"Rufus, what are you doing out of your house?" Henry asked. "It's the only safe place for you now."

"Mother's ill," Rufus replied without looking up. He was feeling through the powdery snow for a specific item. He needed the biggest drill his father owned.

"Don't you think you should be at home looking after her then?" Arabella said.

Rufus paused. "She has Pinrutian flu."

Arabella gasped.

"Come out of there, Rufus," Henry said, more gently now. "We'll all go to her, make her comfortable."

"You know as well as I do, the only cure is sunflower tonic," Rufus muttered. His hands had closed on something large with sharp serrated edges.

"Sunflower tonic is not for the likes of us," Henry said. "Turnip soup is good for the flu. And if we can just sit it out until your father returns, then maybe . . ."

Rufus pulled the enormous drill out of the snow. He clambered back up onto level ground to stare at Henry with angry eyes.

"Turnip soup is good for nothing," he said. "And I can't afford to wait."

"But you'll never get into the sunflower vault, Rufus," Arabella insisted, her voice quaking.

"I have to try." He was walking in the direction of the digging fields now, hefting the huge drill in his hands.

"Don't be so stupid, boy!" Henry called after him. "Tullock will kill you."

"He's killing us all anyway," Rufus said. "One way or another."

And he started to run.

FORTY

# Rufus the Brave

Rufus crunched across the great expanse of the digging fields, his cloak drawn tightly around him. It was dark now and the snow fell like gray petals. It would have been easy to get lost were it not for the pale glint of Hammer Squad armor.

He walked as near to the sunflower vault as he dared. He reckoned the night would hide him from the guards as long as he stayed at a safe distance. Swiftly and silently, Rufus prepared the drill. He flicked a button behind the main drill head, and eight extra cutting attachments shot out from the bit like a spider extending its legs. This was a device his father often used to chomp through ice and earth quickly, to reach buried minerals useful for making his fans.

But Rufus was not digging for minerals. He was digging for his mother's life. He didn't stop to think how plausible his plan was, or to dwell on just how petrified he was. He simply concentrated every fiber of his being on winding the drill into the ground.

Snow flew up and around him, almost blinding him. Then the drill penetrated the layer of ice that formed over the fields during the night and spat chunks of it in all directions—and so on into the hardened earth, the sharp edges churning it like butter.

As the soil became loose, Rufus used the trowel he had brought to spread it thinly around the burgeoning hole. Hours wore on. The hole deepened and widened until Rufus found his head was just below the level of the fields at last. Now he could start to drill sideways. But as he began, the drill bit suddenly hit a large rock and came to a jarring halt, sending a shock wave up the handle and into Rufus's cold hands.

"Argh!" he cried out before he remembered he was not at his workbench now. He bit on his lip and swore silently at himself. That had been loud. And after he'd been so careful to be quiet with the drill!

He levered himself up onto tiptoe. Sure enough, Rufus could just make out through the darkly falling snow that one Hammer guard had prized himself away from the others and was walking toward him, his helmet swiveling left and right. Rufus ducked back down. His heart banged against his rib cage as he imagined the Hammer guard swinging a hammer down on his head. He could hear the footsteps getting closer, crunch, crunch, crunch.

Rufus looked up. The guard was standing on the very edge of his hole, looking about himself, rattling his hammer against his chest plate. But he didn't seem to realize what lay immediately before and beneath him.

Rufus breathed in and out as softly as he could. Surely the guard could hear his heart pounding away; it was certainly thudding loudly enough in his own ears. He twisted his sun-shaped cuff links and hoped against hope that the guard wouldn't even consider taking one more step.

Then, just as Rufus was thinking the guard had taken up a permanent new position, the hefty metal boots turned and crunched away back to the vault. Rufus sighed with relief as he allowed himself a tiny peek over the lip of the hole and, satisfied that danger had passed, continued his drilling and shoveling.

Rufus was sure he could hear voices, a distant babbling that fluctuated above and below the sound of the grinding drill. He stopped. He shuffled backward along his muddy tunnel, climbed out and looked up. Night had given way to the slate gray of morning. Two faces framed in woolen hoods suddenly appeared at opposite sides of the hole. For a horrible, stomach-flipping moment Rufus thought he'd been discovered.

But— "You're crazy," Henry hissed.

Rufus smiled up at him, relieved.

"Runs in the family," he admitted.

"We've managed to swap our digging patch with the people who normally work here," Arabella said as she threw down a couple of cooked turnips and a jar of water.

"Means we can watch over you," Henry added. "Let you know when it's safe to dump loose earth up here."

There was a pause.

"We went to see Elizabeth last night," Arabella said eventually. She bit her lip and glanced across at Henry and then back down at Rufus. "She's not good."

Rufus held her gaze for a moment, and then he turned and crawled back along his dark tunnel to resume his excavating.

Henry and Arabella remained true to their promise throughout the day. But it was obvious they were in a state of high alert. It was so difficult to tell which direction the Hammer Squad were looking in behind their grim helmets. They dug for turnips as usual, but Rufus knew their hands shook all the while.

It was almost a relief when the light began to fail and they could leave the fields and return home.

"Good luck, boy," Henry hissed down the hole at Rufus.

But Rufus was so focused now he barely heard. He worked throughout the night.

As morning came again, Henry and Arabella set about their dangerous vigil once more.

Rufus had lost track of time by now. He thought only of reaching the vault. He just hoped he was still going in the right direction. Then, out of nowhere, the drill was scraping at metal. It ground to a screeching halt. With a thrill, Rufus realized that he'd reached the casing for the telescopic machinery that elevated the vault above the cloud layer. He could hear the machinery compressing inside with a deep rumbling. He'd been underground for many hours since daybreak so he was certain the vault must be descending. It was time to drill upward—but he would have to be careful to wait until the vault was back on the ground.

When the hissing and clanking of the machinery ceased, Rufus twisted his sun-shaped cuff links for luck as fear flickered in his stomach. Would he be heard now breaking in, after getting so far? If he was, it would mean a horrible end for him . . . and his ill mother.

He wound the drill more slowly as it broke through the earth's icy surface into—thin air. Rufus was confused. Where was the vault? He pushed his head and shoulders out of the ground and looked around. The guards were there at their posts, their backs to him, thankfully.

With a sudden, sickening realization Rufus looked up. The vault was just feet above his head, hurtling down toward him—the last part of its descent evidently dealt with by gravity instead of grinding machinery. Rufus's head was like a grape under a stone slab. He gasped and ducked back down as the vault slammed into place, stopping just a hair's breadth above him.

Once his heart had stopped hammering and his ears ringing, he began to bore through the wooden floor above him. As he clambered as quietly as he could through the splintered floorboards into the greenhouse, he took delight in the delicious warmth that lingered there. But the real joy was in the vibrant yellow of sunflower petals all around him.

## FORTY-ONE

# Madeline's Tears

Without the cart to hold him back, Turnip had quite a turn of speed. For hours he thundered across the desert, impervious to the odd whirling dust devil. Madeline hunched against his neck, clinging to his mane, which was matted with sand, while her father gripped the reins behind her. She squinted at the horizon through her dark tinted sunglasses. It was rippling in the heat, but she could just make out a lone figure on a midnight stallion.

"We must keep up with Tullock if we're to find out how he gets across the glacier!" Madeline yelled as she tried to disentangle her wind-whipped hair from her glasses.

"I just hope Turnip's up to it!" her father yelled back.

The poor horse was bathed in sweat—they all were, without the fans to help them—but he galloped on as though sensing his riders' urgency.

It wasn't long before they saw Tullock urge his mighty

stallion through the sheer wall of falling snow into the suffocating gray of the Pinrutian domain.

But Turnip was slower than Tullock's muscular steed at the best of times, and with two riders on his back it was a while before Madeline and her father also approached the harsh divide between sun and snow.

As they passed, Madeline glanced sideways at the border house, half frozen, half baked. It was quite a way off, but she could see that the wall had been patched up already.

Turnip plowed headlong into the falling snow. Snowflakes began to settle on his mane, on Madeline and then on her father. Visibility fell abruptly—as did the temperature. Madeline removed her sunglasses and let them drop into the snow. She felt a twinge of sadness but shook it off—all she could think of now was home. She began to shiver, and her father pulled two colorful striped blankets from a saddlebag.

"Souvenirs from Tresedira," he said as he passed one to Madeline and wrapped the other around himself. "At least we came back with something," he added.

Tullock's stallion had left heavy hoofprints in the snow, but they were rapidly disappearing as more fell.

Philip prompted Turnip into a canter.

The trail led around the glacier in a wide arc to a half-hidden path that went steeply up and over the south face of the mountain.

Madeline felt giddy as she watched the snow plummet into the dark ravines that fell away on either side of the narrow pass. The wind whipped and howled at them as they made their way along it. A couple of times Turnip almost lost his footing and Madeline's heart leaped into her mouth. But eventually, after several hours, the path started to drop down and widen, making progress less perilous.

It wasn't long before they left the rocky trail and were rushing through trees. Daylight was fading now, and the wood was nothing more than a dark web of wintry limbs.

Madeline and her father looked around and tried to get their bearings.

"We're almost home," Madeline said.

The familiar surroundings were comforting, but at the same time they seemed so gray, so . . . sunless.

With a snapping of twigs, Turnip broke free of the wood and started to trot across the fields. They had lost sight of Tullock by now, but it didn't matter anymore. Madeline felt a sudden weariness sweep over her. She just wanted to see Rufus and her mother. The trip had been a failure and she felt somehow as if it was her fault. It was she who had failed.

Madeline's eyes swept across the fields, taking in the scrabbling workers. She noticed that her father also scanned the landscape with thoughtful eyes. He was suddenly quiet and withdrawn.

The snow fell heavily.

In a vain attempt to lift her spirits she glanced across at the soft glow of the sunflower vault. She jolted upright in the saddle. "Rufus!"

Her father followed her gaze.

There he was—inside the vault, filling his pockets with sunflower heads, his face and hands streaked with dirt.

The Hammer guards were only feet from him, but every one of them faced outward, unaware of the larceny taking place behind their backs. At that moment, almost as if he had heard his sister speak, Rufus looked up and saw her too. He seemed to smile, then waved her and their father away urgently. The slightest hint of suspicion among the guards and his fate would be sealed. Madeline gave her brave brother a fierce nod and they rode on.

As they passed through the fields, Madeline noticed that a few of the workers were watching Rufus surreptitiously too. She was surprised and grateful that they weren't blowing the whistle on him, but it was more than that—there was something different about the way their eyes shone and they anxiously clenched their fingers every time a guard shuffled.

Still, Madeline could not ignore the fact that there was only one reason anyone would risk their life to get into the sunflower vault. With a gnawing feeling in her stomach, Madeline hugged Turnip's neck and hoped the exhausted horse still had enough energy to get them home as quickly as possible.

But when they got there, Madeline nearly fell off Turnip's back. For home was there no more. She watched as her father slid off Turnip and circled the snow-filled shallow hollow where his family house had once stood. She chewed on the nail of her little finger and swallowed hard.

"He did it," her father whispered.

"But where's Mother?" Madeline said. Philip looked up, his face white. Life without his home he could just bear, but life without Elizabeth, his children growing up without their mother . . .

Madeline could see the pain and guilt in her father's face.

"It's not your fault," she whispered.

But as they'd been talking, the flow of workers returning home from the fields had begun. Suddenly Rufus sprinted from their midst.

"We must hurry!" he said as he flung his arms about his sister, then his father. "The house is all right. But let's go! It's not good to hang around here."

"What about Mother?" Madeline asked as she followed her brother. It was so good to see him alive and well, but the way he avoided her eyes now made her throat constrict further.

"Come on!" Rufus urged.

"Does she have the flu?" Philip insisted as he ran, Turnip's reins in his hands.

In answer Rufus looked down at a sunflower head peeking from his pocket before ramming it deeper in.

"But did you sell all the fan machines?" he asked breathlessly as he dodged between the forest tree trunks.

It was Philip's turn to look away. Madeline caught her brother's gaze.

"I'll tell you later," she said as her brother's shoulders slumped even further.

Then suddenly their house stood before them, large and incongruous in the clearing, but whole. Madeline felt a rush of warmth—here was something familiar in a world gone awry.

"How . . . ," she began.

"No time to explain." Rufus shook his head.

"But I see you locked it down all right," their father said, casting his eyes over the metal plating that covered the windows and doors. "Pretty simple, wasn't it?"

Rufus glared at his father. "Actually we had a few teething problems." Then he jumped up onto the banister of the veranda and pulled the defense activation lever.

The plating folded away.

Rufus pushed through the door and ran up the stairs two at a time.

"Mother!" he called.

The candles had melted to nothing and the fire had burned out in the grate, leaving the bedroom dark and cold. Madeline stepped into the room behind Rufus as their father rushed around the bed to their mother's bedside.

"Lizzie," he said.

Her skin was bone-white and the snowflake-shaped bumps stood out in stark contrast, a deep blue. She was as still as stone. Philip pressed the back of his hand to her icy cheek, then bent over and squashed his ear to her chest. He could hear nothing.

"Lizzie?" Philip repeated. He knelt and his head fell forward onto her shoulder. "What *have* I done to you? Why did I ever leave?"

Rufus felt his younger sister's hand creep into his. He turned and saw her face wet with tears—Madeline never cried unless it was really bad.

"I'm too late," he said, pulling the sunflower heads from his pocket with his other hand and letting them drop to the floor.

## FORTY-TWO

# Guilt on a Galleon

Sebastian clutched the large leather satchel tightly. His future wealth lay inside it. Although a curious feeling of shame had made him clumsy while sweeping the shelves and surfaces of the fanmaker's borrowed workshop, he was sure he had many tools of superior craftsmanship that were sure to fetch an excellent price.

It had been a difficult journey south through the desert to the port of Whistlehead—he had been forced to hook up with nomads and trade outlandish stories for food and shelter against the unforgiving sun. But now he and Mesmer were taking a long sea voyage, eastbound on a galleon, headed for the rain-lashed region of Pluverton once more and wisely circumventing the snow and ice of the Pinrutian domain. Sebastian had tricked his way on board, carrying a barrel, head down, rags briefly covering his fine though shabby clothes, and now he was guffawing and exchanging stories with the well-to-do fee-paying passengers.

He glanced up at the blossom-white billowing sails and watched the setting sun reflect off the water in splashes of gold. Dolphins swam alongside, keeping apace with the surging vessel.

"Just the two of us once more, Mez!" he exclaimed. "And once we've gathered our fortune, we'll venture far south and distance ourselves completely from the alarming weather at this top end of the world."

But Mesmer's disapproving eyes stared up at him from under his blue furry fringe. The dog stood and skittered to the other side of the deck. "What's up with you, grumpy?" Sebastian called after him.

He suddenly felt very alone. As he closed his eyes and felt the salt spray on his face, memories visited him like long-lost relations.

He had once chartered a boat and sailed up the Ekansey river with a cargo of shoes ordered and paid for up front by the barefooted people of Dumoaty who had, unfortunately, had their own footwear eaten by moths.

However, he hadn't checked the merchandise sold to him, admittedly at a surprisingly low price (though how could he resist such a tidy profit margin?). Anyway, it turned out all the shoes were for left feet only. Sebastian winced as he remembered trying to make a quick getaway upriver with such small sails and a feeble following wind, while dozens of shoes, all of them left, were hurled at him from the riverbank.

Then there was the scandal of Tweehoot. He had sold four dozen sacks of sugar to their mayor for their famous annual cake festival. But the sugar had turned out to be salt. In fact, he'd known that all along. It had taken all of his ingenuity and energy to escape that time. The four chefs of Tweehoot were still looking for him, apparently.

And then there had been the disastrous delivery to Captain Edwin Gold-Thumb's hideout. If only they hadn't insisted he join them for dinner, he would have been well away before they discovered that every other barrel was beetroot juice instead of the promised rum. He had barely escaped with his life on that one—and not without some irony, for he and Mesmer had rolled away from the encampment in one of the empty barrels. There was nothing worse than a gang of irate but sober pirates.

There was no getting around it, wealth was the most important thing to him. And he didn't care how he pursued it. He was as obsessed as Philip Breeze had been with his machines . . . but at least the fanmaker had a family to care for and who cared about him when all else failed. What did he have, other than a small blue dog?

And his guilt. He had enticed Philip and Madeline away from their family and not only made a mess of the whole enterprise, but then abandoned them in their time of need. He liked the Breezes too. Madeline in particular. It was easy to run away from angry pirates and not feel too bad about it, but the Breeze family had style and grace in the face of overwhelming adversity. They'd looked out for him and Mesmer, like on the glacier. He had to admit it—they deserved better.

Sebastian opened his eyes. Mesmer was watching him carefully from the other side of the deck. Sebastian went over to him and sat down quietly.

"Let's not fall out, Mez," he said. "I'm sorry I'm such a rat. Here, take a look at these tools. We're going to make a mint in Pluverton." Mesmer whined as Sebastian drew the beautiful tools from his bag. Their brass elements shone in the glow of the setting sun. He frowned. There was something else in the bottom of the bag. It felt like a book.

FORTY-THREE

# The Fanmaker Begs

It was the tiniest of tremors. It was all the energy Elizabeth had left in her body. But it wasn't wasted.

"Look!" Madeline cried. "Her hand!"

The little finger on Elizabeth's right hand was moving a hair's breadth up and down.

"Get a mortar and pestle," Philip said. "We'll mix up the tonic right here."

Rufus flew down the stairs. The recipe was well known in Pinrut. It was the mantra of all those who had ever seen a loved one fall prey to the Pinrutian flu, even though ordinary people had never been able to put it into practice until now.

Madeline pressed the bright petals and ground the seeds into powder. Rufus gathered the other ingredients and mixed them together in a small cup.

"More syrup than that," Madeline said. "The sugar in it has to act as an energy boost."

"But too much syrup and it will disrupt the nutrients in the petals," Rufus said.

"*Half* a clove of garlic," Madeline urged. "A whole one will kill off the bacteria we need in the sunflower seeds."

"No, no, a whole one," Rufus insisted. "Her immune system is at zero. We don't *want* any bacteria." He paused. "Let's try three-quarters."

But it was their stricken father who pressed the cup to their mother's icy lips. The thick golden liquid pooled in her mouth until he massaged her slender neck to help the tonic down. He ran his hand through his hair and let out a long, ragged sigh. "And now we wait."

But it didn't take long.

Rufus and Madeline could barely believe what they were seeing. One minute their mother was pale and frozen, the next she was sitting upright, her eyes shining and her skin clear and glowing with health.

"I can feel warm sunlight coursing through my veins," she said wonderingly. "Thank you, Rufus." Their father rushed over and held her. She hugged him tenderly. "The adventurers return. Are we rich?"

Philip couldn't answer, so Madeline shook her head solemnly in response. Her mother gave a sad little smile.

"No matter," she said. "We were already rich; we had each other. It just took a strange man and a blue dog to make us realize it."

"A bedside vigil. How touching," someone suddenly sneered.

Rufus and Madeline spun around to see Tullock filling the door frame, his features contorted with rage, One-spike and Three-spike at his shoulder. Their father did not lift his gaze from their mother. Rufus swore under his breath. How could he have been so stupid as to have left the defenses unlocked?

"So this house still stands!" Tullock bellowed. "Furthermore, my manservant is dead and it would appear there has been a theft from my vault!"

Tullock's black eyes flashed to the remains of the sunflowers poking from Rufus's pocket. Madeline suddenly feared for her brother.

"Punishment!" Tullock roared. But then he breathed deeply and continued quietly. "That's what you're expecting, isn't it? Behead the boy or feed him to the octopuses, maybe cast him onto the glacier." Rufus did his best to appear composed and brave, though his heart was hammering.

"No. You Breezes don't deserve such notable deaths. The additional money you owe me for the sunflowers means you'll never be able to make your loan repayments. So your house is mine now, and I'm casting you out into the blizzard tonight. You'll all have perished by morning."

"But I'll work in your fields," Philip said quickly.

"No—" Madeline and her brother began simultaneously.

"And I'd be grateful if we could rent one of your dwellings with some of the money I make digging. The rest would go to you—for the rest of my life," their father went on.

Rufus and Madeline exchanged forlorn looks. Their mother frowned.

But Tullock was enjoying himself. "Demanding, isn't he?" he said mockingly to Rufus and Madeline. "But as I'm a reasonable fellow—yes, Windy, you may work in my fields and I'll find you one of my wondrous abodes, though sadly I believe all the ones with fireplaces have been taken."

"Just don't hurt my family," their father begged.

"You've hurt them yourself with your ridiculous dreams," Tullock snapped.

"At least he *could* dream," Madeline said, her amber eyes shining with defiance once more.

"And look where it's got him," Tullock sneered. "See you first thing tomorrow in the fields, Windy. It was always going to be this way."

And with that Tullock and the two Hammer Squad members clattered down the stairs and left the house. Philip leaned forward and kissed their mother's hand. Madeline and Rufus looked at each other.

"There's no other way," their father whispered, as though sensing their reservations.

"What about Grandfather's notebook?" Rufus ventured.

Madeline held her breath as their father sat seemingly frozen for a second. At last he nodded. "It's time. I owe it to you all."

"Are you sure, Father?" Madeline asked. "The sun could still return. We can make more fans." Or was it truly hopeless now? Her answer came from his.

"Yes, I'm sure," he replied. "Pass it to me, Madeline, please. It'll be in our knapsack, the one I strapped to Turnip's saddlebag. It's over there."

Madeline rummaged for a moment in the knapsack and then looked up with dismay.

"Father, it's not here. I think Mr. Silver must have scooped it up when he took the tools."

# FORTY-FOUR

# Freezing Soil, Aching Hands

Sebastian wiped some ocean spray from the cover and opened the notebook. Intricate plans and drawings, of exquisite detail, filled the pages. It had to belong to the Breeze family. Mesmer gave a little whine of recognition. The old Sebastian would simply have discarded it. But the Breezes had affected him in some mysterious way, and rather than lobbing the book overboard Sebastian turned it over and over in his hands, thinking. It was then that he noticed the curious compartment on the back. He unlocked it with the attached key and read the note within. And although the galleon was sailing on smooth seas, he suddenly felt as though the whole world was trembling on its axis. Could what he had read be true?

Mesmer looked up at him with concern and pawed his shin.

"This secret is too big for just you and me, Mez," Sebastian said.

• • •

Tullock sat astride his stallion, his laughter booming through the silence of the falling snow and across the Pinrutian digging fields. He couldn't help himself. The one man who had fought so long and hard to defy the Tullocks was kneeling before him at last. Bartholomew Tullock had it all—complete power. He owned everything and everyone.

"For the first time in your life you're about to do a day of *real* work, Windy!"

"And what would you know about that?" Philip replied.

Tullock lashed out with a heavy leather boot and kicked Philip into the snow.

"You won't last a week out here," Tullock spat. "But have no fear. When my Hammer Squad carries your lifeless body away, I shall make sure your wife and children take your place."

"You stay away from my family!" Philip yelled as Tullock turned his stallion and cantered away across the fields.

Philip plunged his gloved hands into the ground. The surface ice cracked painfully under his fingers, and he rummaged in the crystallized earth for something that could be construed as a vegetable. With a grunt he pulled out a withered turnip stump. He tossed it into his empty barrel. It rattled around in the bottom like a pea in a barn. It was going to be a long day. He dug down again and wrapped his fingers around another.

"Those children of yours are just dazzling."

Philip looked up. Arabella was walking past on the way to her digging patch.

"Yes, they are," he replied.

"That was quite something, Rufus getting into the vault. There's also talk of how he saved people from Tullock's octopuses. And there's rumors that your Madeline defeated the glacier and the border guard."

Philip sat back and nodded.

"If ever there was a future for Pinrut, it lies with those two children of yours," Arabella added.

Philip agreed. "As long as they don't end up like me," he said.

"Ah, you'll do all right, Philip," Arabella said with a knowing smile. "Sure, you're a sensitive, creative sort, but you're also a stubborn ox."

Philip gave a grim smile and plunged his hands into the freezing soil once more.

"How was it, Father?" Madeline asked as he stepped into their small, chilly hovel that evening. Tullock had done them proud. The place was dank and drafty, bare and dark, and it smelled of rotten vegetables.

Madeline tried not to think lovingly of their old home—probably flattened by now.

"Easier than making fans . . . ," he replied. He rolled his shoulders and rubbed the base of his spine. ". . . Kind of."

"But you're still going to make fans too, Father, aren't you? In the evenings?" Rufus urged. "We don't have to give up *altogether.*"

Philip said nothing. He flopped down into a dilapidated chair and pulled off his woolen gloves, which were practically in tatters. After only one day in the fields his hands shook and his fingers were rigid and bent. He hid them quickly from view.

"Well, *we're* going to keep on making fans," Madeline declared.

"No!" Philip said suddenly. "No more fans. That was my mistake. Study hard. Keep your head down. There are better jobs you can do under Tullock, if he'll have you. Someone has to polish his mountains of silver or clothe his loathsome body."

"I will *never* bow and scrape to Tullock," Rufus fumed.

"Nor me!" Madeline blurted.

Philip looked at their mother—a smattering of pale blue freckles on her face were all that remained of the malevolent illness she had survived. He let out a long sigh.

"Are you hearing this?" he asked as he left the room. "We've raised a couple of rebels."

"Maybe they're just sad to see your passion die," she whispered after him.

That night as their parents slept in one of the tiny, damp bedrooms, Madeline and Rufus laid out the various materials they had managed to scrounge and gather that day—pieces of wood, metal, glass and cloth.

"Let's think of a simple design," Rufus whispered. "So we can make lots of them quickly. Any ideas?"

Madeline thought of the beautiful sun-powered fan her father had made in Tresedira. "Oh, yes!"

Rufus remembered the ingenious way their old house had folded down and then out again. "Me too!"

Suddenly they were aware of a figure watching them from the corner of the room. They spun around, expecting an angry rebuke from their father. But it was their mother standing there. She smiled.

"Can I help?" she whispered.

Dumbfounded, Madeline and Rufus nodded slowly.

# FORTY-FIVE

# The Terrible Truth

Madeline had just said good-bye to her father and watched him walk off dejectedly toward the field for another hard day when she saw them. Through the thick snowfall she could just make out a shivering man in a large hat and an equally cold-looking blue dog. They were circling the empty space where the old Breeze house had once stood.

"Mr. Silver?"

Sebastian spun around and took in the tin hovel Madeline stood at the door of with dismay. "I don't know about you, but I'm beginning to miss the desert," he joked sheepishly as he crunched across the snow toward her, Mesmer trotting anxiously at his heel. But Madeline's cold glare did not melt.

Sebastian began to gabble. "I . . . I've come back to help, to really help this time. And then I'm going to go and make amends to *all* those I've let down—though it will be, er, a rather long journey . . ."

A smile began to defrost Madeline's features. "So, Mr. Silver." She bent down to scoop up the frost-encrusted Mesmer, who wagged his tail delightedly. "It seems I was right, after all. You are a good man, deep down."

"Er, thank you," Sebastian bowed. "But—"

"I thought I told you *not* to come back." Madeline's mother stood angrily in the doorway behind her. But before Madeline could say anything, Sebastian plucked Clement Breeze's notebook from his pocket and held it aloft.

"Please, Mrs. Breeze, hear me out," he said. "I have come into possession of the most awe-inspiring, epoch-defining, world-changing information. I have come all this way to impart it to your family. There's no time to waste."

Inside the unlocked shallow recess in the back of the notebook was a folded letter from Clement Breeze, Madeline and Rufus's grandfather. Sebastian told them to read it—immediately.

Dear Philip, my son,

If you are reading this now, looking for answers, looking for a final hope, I apologize with all my heart, because whatever predicament you find yourself in, I am partly to blame. I was greedy. I had my house, my family, my business, but I believed the Tullocks offered me such riches, such fame, that I could not refuse.

The young Tullock, Bartholomew, wanted to experience snow for a day. He was obsessed. And as I was the expert on all things cool, I was summoned to the Tullock mansion to see what I could do. The challenge appealed to my vanity as a Breeze fanmaker. I would make the greatest fan mechanism ever—one to change the very weather. And I would make it clever, and I would make it well.

It took months of secret visits to the Tullock workshop—oh, but it was so beautiful when it was finished.

The Tullocks paid for the most expensive components imaginable. I had seven centripetal rose-hubs (seven, Philip!) working together, driving counter-rotating turbines, fanning warm air from a furnace across the stretch of ocean just behind the Tullock mansion.

Massive atmospheric clouds formed within moments of me switching it on. Then more fan heads, immense ones (so powerful but oh so delicate!), began to lower the temperature of the clouds to that essential for snowfall. All other weather fronts were simply blown away.

The day the weather machine was switched on was astounding. It was like an arm wrestle with

Mother Nature. A giant whirlwind engulfed the land and sky for miles around, sucking up and freezing anything in its path. Ordinary rain became sleet, and when the sun tried to break through, I turned up the power and the clouds only thickened. Things froze on the spot. Pinrut changed in an instant—cloaked in artificial winter. Bartholomew was delighted.

I had succeeded and earned my fortune. Or so I thought.

For when I went to turn my giant fan machine off, and let normal weather resume, the Hammer guards stepped in front of me and I was informed that the machine would NEVER be switched off.

How could I have been so naive? The Tullocks had always hated our success—and this was their greatest revenge. My greed and passion for acclaim had blinded me.

Of course, the Tullocks loved the snow. The constant cold and gray broke wills, and their money had new power to corrupt people.

Trade ceased—it seemed no one could get in or out of Pinrut. So little would grow in the cold, they soon had a complete monopoly on the only available foodstuffs, and jobs, thanks to the hardy turnips growing in their fields. But all this you know.

The Tullocks didn't even pay me. But who could I complain to? My shame has kept me quiet all these years. Under the circumstances I was even forced to accept a loan from them, with the house as guarantee against it. The Tullocks took great glee in what they saw as my fall from grace, but I thought I was being clever. I believed the sun would be back, that eventually my machine would fail. It was not built to last longer than a day . . . and so I carried on, stubbornly making my fans and passing the craft to you.

But my savings will not last much longer . . .

I have made further radical alterations to the house, even more than those listed in this notebook—ask Henry and Arabella Bugle. I didn't want to worry you if I could avoid it. You see, recently, and now, as I lie here succumbing to the Pinrutian flu I unwittingly helped to create, I'm starting to wonder . . . did I make my greatest fan too well?

No—I must be right, the fan will fail, the sun will return, and the Breezes prosper once more. My family will be fine . . .

But if you are reading this, I am wrong, and my stubborn faith will have made things even worse for you.

*The fan is built into the Tullock mansion barometer tower. Its beauty still haunts me.*

*I am sorry I kept the machine a secret from you, my son. And the rest of Pinrut. Forgive me, Philip. I wish I had been stronger.*

*Clement Breeze, your father*

Elizabeth looked up, her face pale with disbelief. "I remember the day the snow began . . . I can't believe Clement . . . Oh, poor Philip."

"It sort of explains the weird weather we encountered on our travels," Madeline said, chewing anxiously on another finger. "All side effects."

"The Tullocks have played the whole town for fools!"

Rufus twisted his sun-shaped cuff links sharply as he spoke, and Mesmer gave a supportive growl. "That fan needs to be turned off once and for all."

Madeline thought the snow outside seemed different now. It had evil intent built into every flake. She nodded. Their mother glanced down at the letter and then at their determined faces. "We owe it to Pinrut," Elizabeth said, and nodded too.

Sebastian swept off his hat. "We'd like to help in any way possible," he said, his brown eyes glinting with a new resolve.

"Mr. Silver, you don't have to, really," Madeline answered softly. "You've done so much already, bringing us this."

"It's the least a friend can do," he answered, and Mesmer gave a short, sharp bark of agreement.

FORTY-SIX

# Rufus and Madeline Take Action!

Rufus crouched down in the snow next to Mesmer as he reached the tree line of the Reffinock forest. The massive, impregnable Tullock mansion lay before them like some motionless beast, its damp sheen illuminated by the pale gray light of morning.

Rufus looked up at the central tower: the one with the door at its base, the steps running up the outside and the four weather dials at its peak—the barometer tower. He noticed now that the snowstorm did indeed seem to swirl around it as though its gray, unrelenting heart were there. On top of the tower something spun at great speed too, making a low droning noise. Rufus had always assumed it was some kind of weather vane. Now he knew better.

"I think you should stay here, Mez, it'll be safer for you," Madeline whispered from behind them.

"What are we going to do about them?" Rufus pointed in the direction of the half a dozen Hammer Squad members who were patrolling the perimeter of the mansion.

"Tricky . . . ," Madeline agreed.

But Mesmer obviously thought otherwise. Suddenly he launched himself forward and tore toward one of the guards, leaping up at the last minute and hitting the guard's breastplate with a *clang!* Completely surprised, the guard fell backward and landed heavily on his backside.

Quickly, Mesmer bit into the leather wrist strap of the guard's hammer and ran off in the opposite direction, dragging the weapon behind him. Within moments he had disappeared into the trees. The guard struggled to his feet and started to follow the tracks.

"Where did that mutt go?" Madeline heard him cry. "You lot, you have to help me! If Tullock discovers I've lost my hammer, I'm finished!"

Grumbling, two Hammer Squad members peeled away from their patrol and trudged after their despairing colleague.

Determined not to waste the advantage the brave blue dog had won them, Madeline and Rufus went into action against the remaining three.

Rufus swiftly packed a snowball—he'd had plenty of practice—and hurled it at the nearest guard, hitting him square in the front of the helmet and knocking him over. The other two jumped to attention and rushed toward the children. Madeline pulled her blowtorch from her toolbelt and gestured for her brother to do the same.

"Let's heat up these ice buckets!" she cried as she charged forward.

Rufus caught the glee in her voice and leaped into the fray.

The guards swung their hammers perilously close to Rufus and Madeline but the brother and sister were quick on their feet, and every time a hammer swished by, they'd duck in and weld two plates together in an elbow joint, or fuse together the metal covering a knee. Within moments the three guards were moving with all the grace of clockwork tin soldiers.

On Madeline's signal, she and Rufus each leaped onto the shoulders of two of the guards and wrenched their helmets around backward. Those two guards went blundering blindly and stiffly into a nearby drift.

The final guard reared up angrily, but then just came to a grinding halt on the spot, his arms outstretched in an attack position, every joint welded solid. Rufus ripped the key from his belt then shoved him over, the impact throwing up a plume of snow. Breathing hard and with fingers still trembling from the tussle, the boy unlocked the main mansion doors.

They hugged the shadows cast by the immense pillars as they traversed the great hall. Madeline tried not to look at the multitude of Scratskin's stuffed creatures that appeared to clamber across the walls.

Clement Breeze's confession letter had a sketchy map of the mansion on the back, so they knew roughly where they were headed. A narrow door somewhere in the northeast corner of the room would apparently take them up a winding staircase to the barometer tower.

Suddenly Rufus had the uneasy feeling he was being watched. He turned to see two glittering eyes glaring at him from a chair by the fireplace on the far side of the hall. Tullock's mother. A chill rippled up his spine to the nape of his neck. She was trying to heave herself out of the chair, her squinting gaze flicking to a bellpull with a small metal hammer dangling from it.

Rufus ran toward her, his shoes clacking on the marble floor. Realizing she didn't have time to reach the bellpull, Aspid scrabbled for Scratskin's dart-pipe on the table next to her and, with her clawlike fingers, pushed a poison dart inside.

"How I wish my beloved Scratskin were here to do this kind of thing," she muttered to herself as she raised the pipe to her wrinkled lips.

Rufus saw what she was doing and swerved. He heard the dark whistle past his ear.

Aspid quickly reloaded as the boy resumed his approach, licking her lips at the prospect of felling this odious young scamp.

"She'll have the whole Hammer Squad down on us!" Rufus yelled out.

He swerved again and a dart narrowly missed his shoulder.

"Catch!" Madeline called as she ripped a large stuffed pike from a grisly pond-life diorama and swung it by its tail across the hall to her brother.

He caught it and the next dart sunk into its side with a *thunk,* spraying up a fine cloud of sawdust.

*Thunk, thunk, thunk!* Rufus used the fish as a shield to reach Aspid, and when he did he wrenched the dart-pipe from her busy fingers and broke it in two.

The old woman looked up at him with pure venom.

"If you think you can somehow 'save' Pinrut, then you are laboring under a big misconception, boy," she snarled, spit gathering at the sides of her twisted mouth.

With a grunt, Rufus lifted a large stuffed boar from beside the fireplace and placed it on Aspid Tullock's lap.

"Now you're laboring under a big pig," he said.

"Get this off me, you worthless wretch!" Aspid began to shriek in piercing tones. She strained to move but she was pinned firmly in place. "Come back here, you worm!"

Rufus ignored the old woman's protestations and ran to join his sister, who had discovered a tapestry depicting a town in the icy grip of a blizzard. Madeline swept it to one side to reveal steps sweeping upward.

Rufus shot across the landing at the top and approached the door studded with dozens of snowflake-shaped rivets. He frowned and puzzled over which tool from his belt to use to open the formidable lock. But Madeline gently pushed him to one side, pulled an old clip from her raggedy hair and opened the mechanism with a deft twist of her wrist. Rufus gave a brief nod of respect—they'd both had to get a lot more resourceful lately.

Once inside the room at the base of the tower, Madeline gaped at the numerous monitoring devices. Glass domes with every view of Pinrut imaginable. Tullock must have watched and relished the snow falling on everything and everyone for years.

But the weather fan was nowhere to be seen. Rufus was already busy looking for clues as to where it might be concealed, and now his gaze dropped to the floor and an extravagant rug there, with a snow scene woven into it.

He dragged it away. Embedded into the floor underneath was a series of hinged triangular wooden panels joined together to make a traditional fan shape. Madeline stooped to help her brother, slipping her fingers into a narrow gap in the end panel. Together they pulled hard and the panels folded up on each other, revealing a large hole in the floor.

And in that dark recess lay the most incredible feat of craftsmanship Madeline and Rufus had ever seen.

"Wow!"

"But Grandfather couldn't have worked on it down in a hole like that," Rufus said as he leaned down and started to rummage around for a lever. There was a low grinding of gears, and the floor began to shift under their feet.

They shuffled back as it opened up like an iris, glass domes slid out of the way and the fan machine rose. Blackened iron encased the furnace part of it, shaped like a coiled dragon. Smoke snorted from its carved nostrils, and thickened glass where its eyes should have been allowed Madeline and Rufus to peek in at the roaring fire within. They could hear the rhythmic beating of twin bellows fanning the furnace-heated air down long pipes to outside—for all the world as if the iron dragon lived and breathed. The tubes and copper pipes that extended from ridges in the dragon furnace's back bent and twisted about one another in a complex, patterned dance. They disappeared into the tower wall behind the furnace, and had to feed up to the giant fans perched at the very top of the tower.

It was magical. Rufus couldn't help it—he walked slowly around the weather machine, making mental notes on the clever positioning of the myriad valves and switches. Madeline too found herself almost bewitched.

Determinedly she shook her head. "Rufus, we have to hurry—we might be discovered at any moment." With a deep breath she raised her claw hammer above her head.

Her brother did the same—and they swung their arms down together.

The impact juddered through their bodies. Springs and valves flew through the air with discordant twangs.

Wincing, Rufus lunged forward with his chisel and snagged a centripetal rose-hub. It whined for a moment and then exploded spectacularly, spitting components across the room and shattering some of Tullock's glass domes in the process. Pipes ruptured, one gushing hot water into the room. Thinking quickly, Rufus focused his hammer swings on the glass eyes of the dragon and Madeline followed suit. As they finally splintered, the water splattered into the furnace and began to douse the flames there—smoke and steam hissed into the chamber until they couldn't see. Breathing rapidly, brother and sister looked at each other. At last the dragon was dead.

Madeline almost felt sorry for it.

Then, over their coughing, they heard a terrible sound: a thump against the double doors and a shriek. "You will suffer for this! I'll have your entrails woven into a tapestry!" It was Aspid Tullock and the Hammer guards.

"Rufus, we have to finish this properly." Madeline pointed toward the external door up toward the top of the tower—and the fan heads themselves. With stinging, streaming eyes they groped their way outside and locked the door behind them. With his blowtorch, Rufus soldered it shut quickly. The fresh, cold air was a relief, but the skies above were swirling strangely as they started up the stone steps.

The weather had gone haywire.

Behind them, the internal doors gave way and the guards flooded the room.

FORTY-SEVEN

# Elemental Chaos

Sebastian cursed under his breath as he felt the icy earth chill and bite into his knees. Another fine pair of trousers ruined. Not to mention the havoc digging by hand was playing with his lace cuffs.

First all that crawling about and hissing, trying to get the fanmaker's attention without being spotted (mind you, he did not envy the delectable Mrs. Breeze the job of telling her husband what his beloved father had been up to), then the indignity of having to slip into Philip's dreary cloak, and now this. But the sudden heat of a stallion's breath on the back of his cloak hood replaced these trivial concerns with a very real flicker of fear. Sebastian hunched down lower and clawed at the frozen ground, wishing it would swallow him up.

"I can see the bottom of your barrel, Windy," Tullock said finally. "And that upsets me."

Sebastian began to scrabble furiously and, to his surprise, actually managed to dig up a small, withered turnip. He flicked it sideways into the barrel. But then he heard a grunt, followed by the hard crunch of Tullock dismounting.

As the tyrant of Pinrut approached him, Sebastian shuffled around in a circle so that his face remained hidden.

"What is going on here?" Tullock barked. "Speak, man!"

"Digging," Sebastian offered with a cough.

In the next moment, Sebastian's hood was ripped away and he found himself staring up into Tullock's glowering eyes.

"Secrets! We have secrets now! Out here in my fields!" Tullock bellowed. "Who are you?"

Proudly, Sebastian stood up, discarded his cloak and brushed the dirt from his fanciful clothes. "My name is Sebastian Silver," he said. "And whom do I have the honor of addressing?"

"Where in the name of all things frozen is Windy?"

"Windy?" Sebastian echoed innocently.

Tullock lunged forward and grabbed Sebastian by the lapels. "Don't fool with me, man!" he barked. "I can finish you in any way I choose."

Sebastian's chocolate-brown eyes suddenly grew hard. "Save your threats, Tullock," he said. "Word is, your barbarous time at the top is coming to an end."

And as if the skies heard him, the very snowflakes in the air seemed to stop. The gray clouds above began to swirl and thrash like paint being stirred in a bucket, and every snowflake that hung over the fields was suddenly whipped up into the quickening maelstrom. Tullock looked about him in panic. Workers everywhere gasped and Sebastian started to grin.

"So that's where that blasted fanmaker is! They will all die for this," Tullock snarled as he heaved himself back onto his stallion and dug his heels into its flanks.

"I stand by the family Breeze and their desire for the light," Sebastian called after Tullock as he rode frantically away. The nearby workers lowered their gaze from the tumultuous sky to Sebastian. Their faces were pale but their eyes were shining.

The steam and smoke billowing from the broken weather machine created just enough confusion for Madeline and Rufus to make some headway up the steps, pressing themselves nervously against the tower wall side, before the guards started on the soldered-shut door. But it was soon bucking alarmingly. They both knew they were trapped now, with guards about to emerge and block the only way back down. Rufus couldn't believe he was being so foolhardy, but Madeline was right—they had to finish the job if Pinrut was to be saved forever. He smiled grimly at his brave little sister as she raced up the steps before him.

The clouds above were churning and swirling, breaking up one minute to let bright sunshine through, then gathering together the next, to render the sky so dark it was like night. Rainbows formed, then faded. The whole chaotic scene had a terrible beauty, and Madeline could barely tear her eyes away.

Then Rufus caught her attention and pointed upward urgently. Madeline followed his finger to the four weather dials at the top of the tower. The four hands on the faces were turning away from snow toward sun with a determined grating noise. Even better, above the dials and atop the tower, spinning, whining fan blades were striking into one another and exploding outward, blasting away into the maelstrom. The fan had finally destroyed itself, without their help.

The ponderous clouds that had hung over Pinrut for so long broke up rapidly. Shafts of golden light suddenly punctured the gloom like glittering knitting needles being pushed through gray wool.

"The sun's so bright!" Rufus cried, shielding his face.

"You get used to it, Ru," Madeline replied joyfully. "And it's so beautiful too—"

But just at that moment a sudden explosion of activity below them distracted them from their success. First, the outer tower door finally gave way with a loud splintering.

But before the clamoring hordes, being screeched at by Aspid, could give chase up the stairs, their father scrambled into sight over the roof and threw himself onto the bottom step, coming between the guards and his children. His face was grim but determined.

"Father!" Madeline and Rufus exclaimed together, half relieved at the sight of him, and half terrified—there was one of him and there were about fifteen guards.

"Stay there, you two," he called over his shoulder. "I will NOT let them hurt you. I should have had the strength and sense to look in that notebook long ago!"

"And I will not let them hurt YOU either—I fully intend to do that myself," a voice roared as the guards were pushed apart from behind.

"Ooh, yes, now the fun will really start," Aspid cackled delightedly.

It was Tullock.

"What have you done, Windy?" His black eyes glowed with hatred as he took a step forward and Philip backed away before him, up the narrow stone stairway toward Rufus and Madeline.

"Just some routine maintenance," Madeline called down jubilantly.

"My father made a mistake," Philip added sadly. "We've corrected it."

"Your father did something useful for once," Tullock sneered. "He became a true storm maker—how much more esteemed than a mere artsy inventor. How I've longed to tell you over the years, how the irony has made me laugh, to watch you fight so hard against the snow your own father sent you. But I feared that this rash behavior was exactly the kind of thing that would ensue if I did."

"He learned his lesson, and so have I! I know what's really important now."

"What rubbish!" Tullock roared. "Your father died with nothing, you have nothing. I still have everything—all the power."

"It's you who has nothing," Rufus called over his father's shoulder as Philip backed into him, and he and Madeline were pressed up toward the shattered dials. "We all have each other!"

"Please, enough of the sickening Breeze philosophy," Tullock snarled. He glanced up at the blue, sunny skies above him in disgust and wiped a sheen of sweat from his forehead. "The simple fact is that I have the manpower, I have the money and you *owe* me. Therefore, you will rebuild my machine, Windy."

On the chipped ledge that circled the top of the barometer tower, Madeline pressed herself against the broken weather dials and winced as her father laughed bitterly. "What with?" Slowly he held up his red, twisted hands. "You've ruined them. They couldn't fix a broken vase."

But Tullock only shrugged. "You can oversee your children while they do the work." Without turning around he gestured back down the steps threateningly, toward his troop of guards. "After all, what choice do you have?"

"Well, I can think of a lot more preferable options the infamous Breeze fanmakers might want to consider," a voice rang out, followed by a loud growl.

Tullock spun around on the stairs. Madeline, Rufus and their father stared. It was Sebastian Silver and Mesmer. They and the rest of the villagers had the Hammer guards surrounded.

## FORTY-EIGHT

# The Rise of Pinrut

"Attack them, you fools!" Tullock bellowed, but the Hammer guards didn't look so sure; they were heavily armed, but they were also heavily outnumbered.

"Don't even try it," one of the villagers yelled, blinking into the sunlight. Rufus recognized him as one of the men he had saved from Tullock's octopuses.

"We've had enough of your bullying. Mr. Breeze was right—we should have stood up to you years ago." The guards' helmets swiveled from Tullock's angry face to the villagers.' They shuffled anxiously, half hefting their hammers. Even Aspid's abusive hissing did little to motivate them.

With a frustrated wail, Tullock suddenly leaped forward and snapped the sun-bound hand from the nearest weather dial and brandished it like a spear at Philip.

"Watch out, Father!" Madeline cried, and Rufus

wrapped a protective arm about her as they pressed further into the wall.

"I'll have your helmets for soup bowls if you don't jump to it right now," Tullock growled over his shoulder at his guards below. Then he lunged. Rufus watched as his father leaped out of the way, only to find himself teetering dangerously on the edge of the tower ledge. As Tullock sneered and thrust again, Rufus gripped the wall behind him and threw out his hand to grab hold of his father and pull him to safety—just in time.

"Argh!" Tullock's charge continued unchecked, his feet slipped off the ledge and he fell.

But not far.

His voluminous cloak caught on the ledge brickwork and held him there, dangling over the long drop.

"Tully!" Aspid wailed.

Madeline, holding her brother and father's hands tightly, dropped to her knees and peered over the edge at him.

"Let me go then!" Tullock spat. "It's what you want." At the base of the tower, the Hammer guards' courage finally failed them—with the prospect of losing their leader as well as their authority, they turned tail as one and clattered down the mansion stairs, out of the front door and out of sight. The villagers cheered.

Defeat flickered across Tullock's face for a moment.

His cloak gave a sudden rip and he slipped another foot downward. Madeline and Rufus exchanged another look, then, together with their father, reached down, grabbed hold of Tullock's hands and shirt and hefted him back onto the ledge and safety. Tullock scrabbled back and leaned against a dial, his breath shallow. Sunshine swept across his face and he closed his eyes against the glare.

The sound of jeering began to babble through the village crowd at the foot of the tower steps; some of them started up them. "Get out of town!" someone cried, and others joined in the chant.

Madeline glanced at Tullock. He suddenly looked so small and unsure. She felt strangely sorry for him despite all the terrible things he had done.

"You've ruined everything," he spluttered.

At that moment, Tullock's black carriage clattered into the mansion drive, skidding strangely from left to right. The tyrant's mother was perched in the driving seat, struggling with the reins.

"Get in!" she shrieked and her ear-splitting voice traveled up, up, up to the towers far above.

"Let him go," Madeline called down the steps to the villagers beseechingly.

"We're better off without him," Rufus agreed.

Tullock didn't need to be told twice—he scuttled cautiously back down the stone stairs. The villagers parted coldly as he passed.

Minutes later, he emerged from the mansion doors below and dived into the carriage.

"I miss Scraaaatskinnnn," Aspid could be heard wailing as the carriage sped away, the frothing stallions rocking it from side to side unevenly.

Mesmer's joyful yapping led the cheers.

Madeline, Rufus and their father headed down the steps to join everyone. "I have an apology to make on my father's behalf to the town of Pinrut," Philip began cautiously when he reached the bottom step. Madeline slipped her hand supportively into his.

But at a nod from Sebastian, Arabella piped up. "Mr. Silver here has told us everything, and we understand. After all you Breezes have done for us recently, you've more than made up for Clement's unfortunate mistake. It was always the Tullocks who were really to blame anyway . . . and us, for not standing up to them sooner." Sheepish nods swept through the crowd.

"And we're ready to buy your fans now, that's for sure," Henry added with a grin.

"We're so hot," someone agreed.

Philip gave a sad shake of his head. "But I'm afraid I have no fans to sell. The ones I had were lost in Tresedira and my hands can no longer make anything of worth."

Shiny with perspiration, the people of Pinrut began to mutter dejectedly. Madeline could barely keep herself from shouting out loud. She jiggled delightedly on her feet, then glanced sideways at Rufus and touched her finger to her temple and her fist against her heart. Rufus solemnly repeated the gesture.

"We think we can help you," he announced.

"Follow us."

# EPILOGUE

Chattering curiously, the crowd followed Madeline and Rufus out of the mansion and back toward the town center. Their father followed also, his brow crinkled with confusion.

Madeline and Rufus ran on ahead, past the frozen cat and seagull just as the ice that encased them melted away.

The cat leaped but, with an indignant shriek, the bird just made a narrow escape.

Butterflies and birds that had been frozen for years were flicking off their icy jackets and fluttering away. Snow was sliding from the rooftops and gathering in slushy piles in the gutters before turning to tepid puddles.

Madeline imagined the metal rooftops were roasting by now and the interiors of the houses would be like ovens.

Outside their tin hovel, their anxious mother stood,

one hand on Turnip's neck. A smile broke over her face as she caught sight of them both, safe and sound. Turnip's shaggy tail swished happily back and forth in the warmth of the sun.

Together, with Madeline chattering to fill her mother in on everything that had happened all the while, they dragged a colorful blanket from inside the house just as the rest of the town reached them. The blanket was laden with mysterious objects.

The crowd murmured. They appeared to be dozens of beautiful-looking silvered pebbles . . . or fans.

As people watched, each fan folded outward automatically and split in two like a clamshell. Then both surfaces divided again. A tiny spring and gear system in the hinge made the four delicate leaves flutter like dragonfly wings. Traces of heat-absorbing vendilium metal laced the "wings," and colored beads, unpicked from the blanket the fans lay on, striped the bodywork. The crowd was captivated.

"We *wanted* to carry on making them, Father," Madeline said anxiously. "We're a family first, but we *are* fanmakers too—there's nothing wrong with that."

There was a long pause. "They're wonderful." He smiled at last.

Rufus and Madeline beamed.

"They're quite something," Sebastian agreed.

Elizabeth slipped her hand into Philip's rough palm. "And I helped them," she said proudly. "Best I could."

With a host of sighs, one by one the fans began to whirr more loudly and lift off skyward.

"They're powered by the sun like your competition fan," Madeline explained. "They're off to charge up properly."

"And the practical foldaway mechanism was inspired by Grandfather's folding house," Rufus added quietly. His father nodded gratefully.

The ethereal machines flew high into the sky until they were just glinting specks while the crowd watched whisperingly.

"They'll be back soon," Madeline said. "Please just stand where you are. One will find you. There's enough for everyone."

The devices returned, sweeping down over Pinrut like blossoms. One by one, each person found a fan hovering at their shoulder, providing a fresh breeze. The villagers sighed with relief and pleasure as one.

Timely as ever, Sebastian grabbed a barrel that was standing to the side of the Breeze hovel and dropped it down by the front door.

"Please, give all you can for these miraculous machines!" he declared. He rummaged in his own pocket and made a show of dropping in a steady stream of gold coins. Madeline's eyes went wide with disbelief, and she grinned as Sebastian shrugged sheepishly.

Within moments Rufus and Madeline were collecting coins hand over fist as their parents watched proudly. Sebastian let out a whoop and threw his big yellow hat into the air. Mesmer leaped excitedly to catch it in his teeth.

And in the wood the Great Snow Bear shambled away, grumbling. This time he would find a proper winter to last him to the end of his days.